A VIEW TO MURDER

A mystery with a devilish sting

ROBERT McNEILL

Published by The Book Folks, London, 2021

Mass market paperback, 2025

ISBN 978-1-80462-317-6

www.thebookfolks.com

This book is the fifth to feature DI Jack Knox. Details about the other novels can be found at the end of this one.

A list of characters featured in this book can also be found at the back.

Chapter One

It was known as 'haar' – the local name for a dense fog that drifted inland from the Firth of Forth. Haar occurred when warmer temperatures in the southern half of the North Sea met Arctic waters drifting south. The result was a bank of thick mist, which entered the Forth Estuary and blanketed the city until the sun rose, causing it to dissipate.

Clare Tomkins was jogging near the cliff edge in Holyrood Park when she saw it roll in from Leith and cover the New Town. A minute later the fog reached Edinburgh Castle, which moments before had been bathed in dawn light.

She stopped, dipped into a bag at her waist, and extracted her iPhone. The haar all but enveloped the city now, obscuring the sun's rays. A few remaining shafts shone on tendrils wreathing the ramparts, giving the castle an ethereal look. Clare thought it made an interesting picture, and raised her mobile and framed the scene.

She clicked the shutter, and was in the act of placing the device back in her bag when she heard footsteps. Visibility was down to a few feet, but she was just able to see someone heading in her direction.

'Who's there?' she said.

The figure grew nearer, but no one replied.

'Who's there?' she repeated anxiously.

The fog lifted a little, and Clare gave a sigh of relief. 'Oh, it's you,' she said. She paused a moment, then added with a hint of irritation, 'Why didn't you answer? You had me worried.'

The person said nothing and continued to advance. Clare studied the individual's face, then her expression changed to alarm. 'No!' she shrieked. 'No-o!'

Once more the fog lowered, and the assault began. A series of vicious blows sent the young woman reeling towards the cliff edge where she lost her footing, slipped, and plummeted 150 feet to the rocks below.

* * *

'Death would have been instantaneous,' Alexander Turley was saying. The pathologist was crouched beside the body, which lay at the bottom of a section of the cliffs, a sill of Carboniferous basalt formed by a long-extinct volcano.

Known as Salisbury Crags and part of Holyrood Park in central Edinburgh, they were accessed via the Radical Road, a ten-foot-wide track that girdled the near-vertical rock face.

Turley and four others – DI Jack Knox and DS Bill Fulton, together with forensic officers DI Ed Murray and DS Liz Beattie – had gained the high point of the path after walking from a car park at Holyrood Palace, 500 feet beneath the ridge.

'Anything point to foul play, Alex?' Knox asked.

'Bit early to say,' Turley replied. 'Quite a heavy mist earlier. The fall could have been accidental.' He swung round to face Knox and gestured towards the inert figure, which lay in a foetal position, dressed in a bright yellow jacket.

'I'd say her spine's broken in a few places,' Turley continued. 'Serious head trauma, too, evidenced by ocular and auricular bleeding. Naturally, I'd have to carry out a full PM before I can rule anything out.'

Murray pointed to the top of the cliff face and nodded to Beattie. 'Liz and I will carry on, Jack. A park ranger with a Land Rover is waiting with two officers from St Leonards. They've sealed the path at the south end. I'll ask him to take us to the top. We'll check back here before Mr Turley leaves.'

'Okay, Ed,' Knox replied. 'Let me know if you find anything of interest.' Then, as the officers moved off, he said to Fulton, 'The couple who found her, Bill, did uniform take their statement?'

'Aye.' Fulton took a notebook from his pocket, leafed through it, and found the page he was looking for. 'Mr and Mrs Graham, 144/29 Dumbiedykes Road.' He waved a hand towards a built-up area facing the cliffs. 'Other side of the park's perimeter wall. A five-minute drive.'

'What did they say?' Knox asked.

Fulton glanced at his notebook again. 'Let's see… both in their mid-sixties, recently retired. Take a walk up here most days, leaving their flat around seven. Told the interviewing officer that this morning they arrived at Hunter's Bog around 7.15am with the intention of walking as far as St Anthony's Chapel. They're in the habit of returning home via this path. Circular route, normally takes them 45 minutes.'

Knox was aware that Hunter's Bog was the name of the valley on the lee side of the cliffs, and that St Anthony's was the ruins of a twelfth-century chapel overlooking Holyrood Palace.

'But they didn't go that way this morning?'

'No, boss.' Fulton thumbed towards the pathologist, who was examining the corpse's eyes with a penlight. 'Like Mr Turley said,' he continued, 'fair bit of haar earlier. Clear when the Grahams left home, but by the time they arrived it was thick.'

'Go on.'

'So they changed their mind. Decided to keep to the Radical Road till they reached the Holyrood Palace end, then turn about and make their way back.'

'Right,' Knox said, glancing at Turley. 'But this was as far as they got?'

Fulton followed his gaze, shaking his head. 'Aye. Not a nice sight before breakfast, eh?'

'No, indeed,' Knox said. 'Okay, we better have a word.' Then to Turley he said, 'Alex, Bill and I are heading off to interview the couple who found her. Okay if I ring you later?'

The pathologist clicked off the penlight and rose slowly, massaging the small of his back. 'Getting too old for this,' he murmured to himself, then, glancing at Knox, said, 'Aye fine, Jack. Murray and Beattie should be back soon.' He checked his watch and added, 'Half-nine now. By the time they finish my lads'll be here to pick up the body… say early afternoon?'

Knox gave an acknowledging nod. 'Afternoon's fine, Alex. Speak to you then.'

* * *

Number 144 Dumbiedykes Road was a three-storey block in an estate built in the 1960s to replace densely packed Victorian tenements which had been condemned and demolished. Knox learned this from Fulton, who gave him a potted history of the area as they drove in from Holyrood Road.

'My grannie and granda were born and raised in Arthur Street,' Fulton told him. 'I remember visiting as a laddie. You should've seen it, boss, I don't think there was a steeper street in town – the gradient must have been one in ten. Delivery drivers had to make sure their handbrake was pulled to the last ratchet, *and* leave their vehicles in gear.

'One day my granda saw what happened when a driver forgot. The man's wagon – a coal lorry – slipped its brake

4

and ran out of control. Smashed through gates near a bowling green at the bottom, ended upside down. No one was hurt, fortunately.' He paused, chuckling. 'But a lot of folk warmed themselves gratis for a week or two that winter.'

Knox glanced over and smiled. 'Your grannie and granda among them?'

Fulton gave a wink and grinned. 'Ah now, boss, that'd be telling.'

The sergeant had just finished speaking when Knox's satnav informed him he'd arrived at his destination. The detectives exited the car and entered the block, arriving at the second floor, where a sign indicated that flats 20–29 were located to their left.

Number 29 was situated near the end of the landing, where Knox's press on the bell push was answered by a small woman with a pale complexion. 'Yes?' she said.

Knox showed her his warrant card. 'Mrs Graham?'

'Yes,' she replied hesitantly.

'Detective Inspector Knox and Detective Sergeant Fulton,' Knox said. 'I believe you spoke to one of our colleagues earlier?'

'Oh – to do with the lassie in Holyrood Park?'

'Yes,' Knox replied. 'Mind if we talk a moment?'

Mrs Graham opened the door, waving them inside. 'I'm not sure we can tell you more than we told your colleague,' she replied, pointing to the end of a short hallway. 'The living room's on the left. Take a seat on the couch.'

The detectives entered and saw a three-piece suite positioned in front of a fireplace, where flames from a gas fire flickered around a couple of artificial logs.

Mrs Graham followed them inside and gestured to the settee. 'Please,' she said, 'sit yourselves down.'

As Knox and Fulton did so, a door at the corner of the room opened and a short, balding man stood wiping his hands on a dish towel. 'We've got visitors?' he asked.

'Aye, Davie,' Mrs Graham said. 'These men are detectives. They're here about–'

'Yes, I know, the girl,' he interrupted. 'I don't understand why you'd want to speak to us again. We went over everything earlier with a young officer at the scene.'

Knox said, 'You're Mr Graham?'

'Aye, sorry,' the man replied, indicating the door behind him. 'I was in the kitchen, drying dishes, radio on. Didn't hear the doorbell.'

'I see,' Knox said. 'Yes, your wife explained about your statement, sir. But we'd like to check again, just in case something was missed. You don't mind?'

Graham shook his head. 'Not if it'll help.' He nodded to the kitchen. 'You'd like a cup of tea?'

'No, thanks,' Knox said. 'We don't intend keeping you long.'

'It's no trouble.'

'That's kind of you,' Knox said. 'But, really, we're okay.'

Graham placed the dish towel on a nearby sideboard and went to one of the armchairs.

As his wife sat on the one opposite, Knox took a notebook from his pocket. 'You told the officer you left home at seven this morning?'

'A minute or two after that, actually,' Graham said. 'I'd just listened to the news headlines on Radio 4.'

'But you arrived in Holyrood Park around quarter past seven?'

His wife nodded. 'Yes, via our usual route; only takes fifteen minutes – St Leonard's Bank to the wee roundabout at the top of Queen's Drive. We crossed there and made for the Radical Road.'

Her husband dipped his head in agreement. 'Aye, as I told your officer, we usually circle round the back of the Crags and head for Hunter's Bog.'

'The fog made you change your mind?' Fulton asked.

'Uh-huh,' Graham said. 'Rolled in in just a matter of minutes. We had barely reached Queen's Drive when it began to thicken.'

'Which is why we decided to forgo Hunter's Bog,' Mrs Graham said, 'it can be quite marshy in places. You've got to be able to see where you're putting your feet. Not the first time I've sunk in up to my knees.'

'Aye,' her husband agreed. 'And I've had to pull you out.' He shook his head, adding, 'We decided not to risk it.'

'Did you see anyone when you arrived?' Knox asked.

'At the Radical Road, you mean?'

'Yes.'

Graham shook his head. 'No, as I told your colleague, the fog was pretty thick then. There was a couple ahead of us, though, when we neared the roundabout. It wasn't as murky then.'

Knox frowned and glanced at Fulton. The sergeant took out his notebook, studied it for a moment, and shook his head.

'You didn't mention that to the officer who interviewed you,' Knox said.

'Didn't we? Maybe because we hadn't reached the park proper.'

'The people you saw, they were definitely together?'

Graham gave his wife a questioning look.

'I'm not sure it was a couple,' she said.

'Male or female?'

'As Davie says, the fog hadn't completely covered the park. But it did obscure the view quite a bit, so I can't be sure. I did see what looked like dark clothing.'

'They were headed towards Hunter's Bog,' Graham added. 'Skirted the track leading to Arthur's Seat, I can never remember its name...'

'The Hawse,' Fulton said.

'Aye, The Hawse,' Graham agreed. 'Wouldn't have been that far over if they were making for the Radical Road.'

'I see,' Knox said. 'You didn't notice anyone else?'

'No,' Graham replied.

'The officer's notes say that you walk there regularly,' Fulton said.

Graham nodded. 'Aye, both keen hikers. Completed the West Highland Way in spring of this year, the Great Glen last summer. Like to keep in shape. We've been members of the Southside Rambling Club since 1998.'

'The person or persons you saw, did you catch sight of them again?'

The Grahams shook their heads and answered in unison. 'No.'

Knox nodded. 'So when you reached the Crags you started along the Radical Road?'

'Yes,' David Graham said. 'The track's only a dozen feet in width. So we stayed in the centre, barely able to see where the path met the grass. Kept going, though, in the hope it would lift.'

'But it didn't?'

'Not till almost nine. We were back here by then.' Graham shook his head and continued, 'No, we carried on up the track to the highest point. Where the Crags face the castle there's a huge fissure – "the Cat's Nick" I think it's called – the girl had landed near the foot.'

'How did you discover her?' Knox asked.

'You mean with the fog and all?'

'Yes.'

'Well…' He gave his wife a questioning look. 'When we heard the noise; we would have been about thirty yards from the Cat's Nick?'

She nodded. 'About that, yes.'

'We thought it was a rock falling,' Graham said. 'Happens occasionally; erosion at the cliff face.'

'Uh-huh,' Knox said. 'Carry on.'

'When we got there,' Graham said, 'I looked in the direction of the crash and saw something yellow. In amongst the rocks, a short distance from the path.'

'Her jacket,' Fulton said.

'Aye, but I didn't know that then.' He motioned to his wife. 'I told Ellie to stay put, and took out the torch I had with me. Walked in a wee bit and came across her.' Graham paused a moment, and went on, 'The girl's injuries… no exaggeration to say they were horrific. I knew immediately she was a goner.'

His wife shook her head, and swallowed. 'When we started out I never thought I'd be grateful for fog. But I was then.'

'And the only thing you heard prior to that was what you thought was a rock falling?' Knox asked.

Mrs Graham pursed her lips. 'When the young policeman interviewed us I was still in shock,' she said. 'But I've remembered something since.'

'Go on,' Knox said.

'When we were approaching the Cat's Nick I heard cries, which I took for a seagull. Only after we made our way home did I realise what I'd actually heard.'

'What did you hear?'

'A girl screaming out loud,' she said. 'Twice.'

Chapter Two

'Fair likelihood our victim was pushed, don't you think, boss?' Fulton was saying. Ten minutes had passed and the detectives had concluded their interview and were back in the car.

'Won't know for sure until Turley completes the PM, Bill, but I agree. And of course, there's still forensics at the scene itself. Murray and Beattie might've found something.'

Knox was interrupted by his mobile ringing. He took the device from his pocket, glanced at the screen, and placed it on the hands-free unit. 'Talk of the Devil.' He switched on the dash speakers and added, 'Ed?'

'Jack,' Murray replied. 'The park ranger took us up to the section of cliffs where the girl fell. Our preliminary examination shows signs of a struggle near a spot called the Cat's Nick.'

As Knox and Fulton swapped glances, Murray continued, 'But there's more. Liz found an iPhone wedged between rocks a foot or so from the cliff edge. It's on the Directfone network, registered to a girl called Clare Tomkins, aged 19. Home address: 44 Upper Newton Grove, Nairn. We checked its address book. One of the numbers is the reception office at the Pollock Halls of Residence, Holyrood Park Road.'

'So she's a student?'

'We think so,' Murray said. 'And in the habit of using the park most days if the images are anything to go by.'

'You checked them?'

'Liz did. Fair selection of photos of the park and surroundings, taken over the last month: Salisbury Crags and the ruins of St Anthony's Chapel; Holyrood Palace and the Scottish Parliament; St Margaret's Loch.'

'Any personal stuff?'

'Uh-huh. Few dozen frames of people her own age, both sexes. Some appear to have been taken in and around the Pollock Halls – dormitories, canteen, recreation areas and the like. Others look like snaps of nights out – pubs, etcetera.'

'Might prove useful.'

'Yeah,' Murray agreed. 'The most recent is the one she took this morning: 7.22am. Shows the castle ramparts wreathed in fog – highlighted by a few beams of sunshine. Pretty impressive picture.'

'Taken from the Crags?'

'Aye,' Murray replied. 'We studied it in detail. At the bottom of the frame you can see an outline of the cliff edge to the right of the Cat's Nick. Which is where we found signs of a struggle. Also near where Liz found the iPhone.'

'So she was attacked immediately after she took the picture?'

'Looks that way. We're guessing from the photo she was standing approximately five feet from the edge.'

'Interesting,' Knox said. 'And the phone – you'll be able to let us have it soon?'

'We've just to check for prints and DNA. Liz or I will drop it off after lunch.'

'Much obliged,' Knox said. 'You're almost finished?'

'Pretty much. We took images and soil samples at the top and are back at the locus now. Other video and photography's almost done; the pathologist's lads have arrived to take the body to the Cowgate.'

'Mr Turley's finished at the scene?'

'Aye. Left fifteen minutes ago.'

'Okay, Ed, Thanks.'

'No problem, Jack. I'll keep you updated.'

* * *

Knox and Fulton arrived back at Gayfield Police Station a few minutes after eleven and were greeted by DC Mark Hathaway and DS Arlene McCann, two other members of Gayfield Square's Murder Inquiry Unit. McCann was a recent appointee to the team, having only recently moved to the city from Gartcosh, Police Scotland's headquarters in west central Scotland.

'Morning, Bill; morning, boss.' Hathaway turned to Fulton and said, 'Sammy at the desk told us a body had been found at Salisbury Crags and you'd been called at home.'

'Aye,' Fulton agreed. 'DCI Warburton rang at eight. Told me the boss was already on his way and to meet him there.'

McCann, a dark-haired woman in her early forties, looked up from her desk. 'Accident, suicide or murder?' she asked.

Knox shrugged off his coat and draped it over the back of a chair. 'We're leaning towards the latter, Arlene,' he said. 'One of the witnesses is sure she heard screams before she and husband found the body. And Murray and Beattie found signs of a struggle near the cliff edge.'

'Ah,' McCann said.

Knox nodded to a door at the corner of the room. 'DCI Warburton in?'

'Yes, in his office,' Hathaway said, adding, 'Oh, I almost forgot. He told me to tell you to see him when you arrived.'

Seeing Knox's mystified look, McCann smiled and said, 'He's not on his own, boss.'

'Really?'

'Uh-huh. Brass. A senior officer I recognise from Gartcosh, DCS Steele, and a pair of scruffy-looking guys I haven't clapped eyes on before.'

'They're in the job?'

McCann shrugged. 'Couldn't say.'

Knox made a face. 'Curiouser and curiouser.'

He went over, tapped at the door, and heard his boss's voice. 'Come in.'

Knox entered and saw four men. Warburton, patrician-looking and in his mid-fifties, sat at one corner of the desk, and the uniformed DCS at the other. Steele was equally distinguished-looking, with salt-and-pepper hair and a neatly trimmed moustache.

The other two sat near the window and looked to be in their mid-thirties. The man nearest Knox wore a denim jacket and jeans. He was ruddy-faced and clean-shaven, his light brown hair styled in a crew cut. He was markedly different from his companion, who was heavily bearded with shoulder-length hair, and wore a leather biker jacket and faded corduroy trousers.

'Jack,' Warburton said, waving a hand towards the senior officer, 'I'd like you to meet Detective Chief Superintendent Andrew Steele. DCS Steele heads Gartcosh's narcotics division.'

Steele inclined his head and extended his hand, which Knox shook. 'Pleased to meet you, DI Knox,' Steele said.

'Sir.'

Steele placed a folder on the desk and said, 'You're probably wondering what this is about?'

Knox nodded. 'I am, sir, yes.'

'You're aware of the shooting of a man at Kaimes Green Crescent last Thursday?'

'Yes, sir. We were told it was drug related. I believe officers from Gartcosh were brought in to investigate.'

'We were,' Steele confirmed. 'And you're right, it is drug-related. The deceased is one Norman Smeaton, aged 29, who we've reason to believe was a pusher for a man called Gus McMahon, a local drug dealer whose fiefdom includes the Kaimes Green district.'

Steele studied Knox for a few seconds, then indicated the folder in front of him. 'I wonder, Inspector Knox, if you recall a man called Bernard Macintosh?'

Knox pondered this for moment. 'The name rings a bell, sir, yes,' he replied.

'Charged with possession of cocaine in 1997,' Steele said. 'Found guilty. Received an eight-month suspended sentence and was fined £500.'

Knox nodded. 'Yes, sir, I remember. I was based at St Leonards at the time. The drugs were found when Traffic caught Macintosh speeding in Newington. A bag of cocaine was found when his car was searched. I interviewed and charged him. I think his brief subsequently persuaded the court that there was no intent to supply; the cocaine was for personal use only.'

'You recall correctly,' Steele said. 'And since 1997 Mr Macintosh has maintained a scrupulously clean sheet: no misdemeanours of any kind – not even a parking ticket. In fact, to all intents and purposes, Mr Macintosh is an upstanding citizen. Runs a successful fruit and veg business – three shops, all in the better parts of town: Morningside, Corstorphine and Stockbridge.' Steele shook his head. 'Except it's a front. Macintosh may appear to have kept to the straight and narrow, but his real business is the same as it was when you charged him in '97 – drugs.'

'He's connected to Smeaton's death?' Knox asked.

'Indirectly,' Steele said. 'I explained the man was McMahon's pusher?'

Knox nodded.

'McMahon has a rival,' Steele said. 'A man called Hugh Wallace. Both are in their mid-thirties. And both are supplied by Macintosh. McMahon oversees a network of pushers in the Kaimes Green and south-east of the city, Wallace does much the same thing west of Comiston Road.'

'You think it was Wallace?'

'We've reason to believe so, yes. Either him or one of his acolytes. A perceived breach of territory, most likely. There's a fair amount of animosity between them.'

'Does Macintosh know of Wallace's link to the murder?'

'We don't think so,' Steele replied. 'Not yet, anyway.' Steele waved in the direction of the men sitting at the window. 'I think before we go further, I'd better affect introductions.' He indicated the man with the crew-cut and went on, 'This is Detective Sergeant Keith Skinner. The bearded chap beside him is Detective Sergeant Steve Hammond. They're members of my team. Both work undercover.'

The men rose, exchanged greetings and shook hands, then returned to their seats.

'We're in the process of setting up a sting designed to put an end to Macintosh's operation,' Steele said. 'But first perhaps I should go into a little more detail.'

He stood and crossed to a whiteboard opposite the window, took a marker pen, and wrote:

1. ?

2. Macintosh

3. McMahon (SE) – Wallace (SW)

4. Smeaton, etcetera

He turned to Knox and said, 'The area of concern here is south Edinburgh, where there are four levels in the chain of Class A drug dealers. As you can see, Macintosh is at number two. He's the regional distributor. The pair at number three buy from him and distribute in the south-east and south-west. Finally at level four are people like Smeaton, selling directly to the end user.'

He waved towards the undercover officers. 'The sting I mentioned is designed not only to drive a deeper wedge between McMahon and Wallace, but also to create a rift between them and Macintosh.

'My undercover officers are currently in the process of gaining their trust. Skinner has successfully hooked McMahon, and Wallace has swallowed the bait dangled by Hammond. Macintosh's dealers have been persuaded my men are players in a big Glasgow narcotics outfit.

'Our aim is to tempt them to increase their profits by cutting out their supplier, Macintosh – and make sure he gets to know about it. Both operations are being orchestrated simultaneously, though McMahon doesn't know about DS Hammond, nor Wallace about DS Skinner.

'If we can make Macintosh think he's being usurped – he just might panic and go and speak to his source. You see, although we've kept tabs on him for months, we've yet to discover who that is.' Steele turned back to the whiteboard. 'Hence the question mark: our wholesaler's identity. Once he's collared, we'll be able to take them all out.' Steele replaced the marker and returned to the desk. 'Which brings us to why I asked to see you. Shortly after Macintosh was cleared in 1997, he wrote us a letter.'

The DCS removed a sheet of A5 paper from the folder and spread it on the desk. 'The last paragraph reads: "I harbour no grudge. In fact, I would like to thank Lothian and Borders Police for the way in which the officers conducted the inquiry, particularly Inspector Knox, who was extremely courteous in his questioning. He treated me fairly throughout."

'I'd like you to help us with the case, Inspector Knox. Begin by interviewing Sandy Purvis – a retired bus driver who witnessed the shooting and was hit with a stray bullet. After that, you can speak to Smeaton's widow. The most important person, however, is Macintosh himself.' Steele tapped the letter. 'He knows and trusts you, and I've an idea if we go about it the right way our plan just might succeed.'

'With respect, sir,' Knox said, gesturing to the note. 'The last time I saw Macintosh was more than twenty years ago. He probably won't remember me.'

'Oh, I think he will,' Steele said. He took the A5 sheet and gave it a little wave. 'I've been in the force almost forty years. Believe me, any villain who goes to the trouble of penning a letter like this…'

'Just to be clear,' Knox said, 'didn't you say you had officers investigating Smeaton's murder?'

'I did, yes,' Steele replied. 'DI Niall Paterson has conducted preliminary investigations, which includes interviews of the aforementioned Mr Purvis, and Smeaton's widow, Lisa. Forensics have been completed at the scene of the shooting, and Smeaton's body has been transferred to Gartcosh, where it's currently being examined by our pathologists.' Steele cleared his throat. 'I don't want it to go further than this room, Knox, but Paterson doesn't exactly have my full confidence. A bit too rough at the edges. A good officer, but not the right man to handle this inquiry. He's the last person I'd want to speak to Macintosh, not if we're to succeed in getting the results we're after. No, I'll inform Paterson that you'll conduct the interview. Tell him to bring you up to speed with his investigations to date.' Steele paused for a long moment, then added, 'What do you say?'

'So the real reason for my seeing Macintosh,' Knox said, 'is to hint that McMahon and Wallace are in the process of cutting him out?'

Steele steepled his hands and gave a little smile. 'Exactly.'

Knox shook his head. 'I don't know, sir,' he said. 'My team and I have just embarked on what I'm sure will prove a murder investigation – a young girl who was found at Salisbury Crags.'

'I don't think you'd be hampered in that,' Steele said. 'You should be able to conduct both investigations simultaneously.' He turned to Warburton. 'What strength is the station's MI team?'

'We're back up to four, sir, not including two forensics officers and myself,' Warburton replied. 'DS McCann joined us last week.'

Steele's brow furrowed. 'McCann,' he said. 'The dark-haired woman I passed on my way in?'

'Yes, sir,' Warburton replied.

'I think I know her,' Steele said. 'She was appointed from Gartcosh?'

'Yes, sir.'

'Uh-huh, I *do* know her. Completed a course on narcotics when she was with us. Proved very capable.'

He turned back to face Knox. 'I'm sure, Inspector Knox, that you'll be able to manage both investigations with the team you have. If you need back-up at any point you can always call on Paterson. I don't think that'll prove necessary, however, as your main interview will be with Macintosh. By the way, make sure DS McCann is with you when you see him – I think you'll find her experience helpful. Report back to me through DCI Warburton.'

Chapter Three

'So we're handling two murder inquiries now?' Fulton was saying. Fifteen minutes had passed, Steele and the others had departed the office, and Knox and his team were seated at their desks. Knox had explained the undercover officers' involvement, the sting, and Steele's desire to see Macintosh's operation closed down.

'We should manage,' Knox said. 'As I explained, the only reason they've brought me in is because I've had dealings with him.'

Fulton shook his head. 'This Macintosh,' he said, 'can't say I've heard of him.'

'You wouldn't, Bill,' McCann said. 'Folk like him go out of their way to keep a low profile.'

'Okay,' Knox said, checking his watch. 'These new circumstances require a rescheduling of manpower.' He motioned towards McCann. 'As I said, Arlene, DCS Steele wants you with me.' Then to Fulton, he added, 'Meantime, Bill, I'd like you and Mark to make a start on the Tomkins investigation.'

Hathaway retrieved a large manila envelope from his desk. 'DS Beattie dropped by with this when you were with the DCS, boss,' he said. 'Told us they're holding onto her iPhone for forensics, but said to tell you the only fingerprints belong to the girl herself. The envelope contains a printout of all personal photographs in her image file.'

'Good, Mark,' Knox said. 'Next of kin informed?'

Hathaway nodded. 'Mother and father. I phoned Nairn Police. They've sent a couple of officers to break the news.'

'Aye,' Fulton said sombrely. 'Always the hardest part. Thank God we seldom have to do that anymore.' He stood and glanced at Hathaway. 'Okay, son, bring the photos. We'll head up there and see what we can find out about Ms Tomkins.'

* * *

Glassel House was one of two U-shaped blocks that stood opposite each other within the Pollock Halls of Residence student complex. The complex stood in twelve acres of ground in the shadow of Arthur's Seat, which was situated in the south-eastern part of Holyrood Park in central Edinburgh.

DC Hathaway called at the secretary's office and was told Tomkins shared dormitory 2c with two other young women, Fiona Baird and Sofia Adler. Glassel House, he was told, was located at the end of a short access driveway off Holyrood Park Road. The detective followed her directions, parked, then he and Fulton walked the short distance to the block, where they found 2c on the second floor.

Fulton's knock was answered by a blonde-haired girl around twenty who spoke with a pronounced German accent. 'Yes?' she said.

'You're Sofia Adler, Miss?'

'Yes.'

'We're police officers,' Fulton said. 'It's to do with your room-mate, Clare Tomkins.'

The girl's face crumpled and tears began to form. 'What people are saying – it is true. She is dead?'

Fulton nodded. 'I'm afraid so, love,' he replied. 'Your other room-mate, Ms Baird, she's here?'

A pretty brunette appeared at Adler's shoulder. 'Yes,' she said. 'Sorry, I was brushing my hair when you knocked.'

'We'd like to ask about Ms Tomkins,' Fulton said. 'It's okay to come in?'

'Please,' Baird said, then her room-mate stood to one side, and the detectives entered. 'Both Sofia and I had lectures scheduled today. But when our tutors heard about Clare, they advised us not to attend.' She swallowed hard, and added, 'Knew our minds wouldn't be on our studies.'

'I understand,' Fulton said.

Adler gestured to a couple of chairs at a table near the window. 'You and your friend will sit down, please?'

'Thank you,' Fulton said. As he and Hathaway complied, he paused a moment, and added, 'Ms Tomkins, how long did you know her?'

Baird sat on the edge of a bed near the detectives and her room-mate took an adjacent stool. 'About a month and a half,' she replied. 'September 16, start of term.'

'You'd formed a friendship?'

Baird nodded. 'You could say so, yes. Sofia, myself and a couple of girls from the adjoining dorm. We've similar interests, hang out together. You know, go for a few drinks, see a movie, do a bit of shopping.'

'Did Clare have a boyfriend?' Hathaway asked.

'I think she dated one or two guys, also students. Nothing serious, though.' Baird gave Adler a questioning look. 'You, Sofia?'

Her room-mate shook her head. 'I'm not sure. She did tell me she had a fall out with one. I can't remember who it was.'

'A falling out, you mean,' Hathaway said, 'an argument?'

'Yes,' Adler said. 'A falling out.'

'These lads,' Fulton said. 'They stay here in Glassel House?'

Baird jabbed a finger towards the floor. 'The dorms below. Ground floor.'

'Do you happen to know their names?'

Baird raised her eyes to the ceiling. 'Let me see… I'm sure one of them was called Fraser. Not sure of his surname. The other one… Danny, Dave.' She shook her head. 'No, I'm sorry.'

Hathaway leafed through the eight-by-ten-inch photographs in the envelope Beattie had given him. Among them he found a couple of prints that pictured Clare with two different young men. The first had thick, curly black hair and ruddy features. The image, a selfie, had been taken in Holyrood Park, as the pair were posed with Arthur's Seat in the background.

The second – also a selfie – had been taken in a bar, as there were beer bottles on a table in the foreground. The man in this image was fair-haired and bespectacled, and he and Clare were pictured raising their glasses to the camera as if making a toast.

Hathaway selected the first print and passed it to Baird. 'The men,' he said. 'Do you see either of them in this picture?'

She took the image and studied it for a moment. 'It's Clare with Fraser in the park. You know, I think I've just remembered his surname. McCauley.' She passed the image to Adler. 'Don't you agree, Sofia?'

Adler looked at the photograph and nodded. 'Yes. I, too, recall this. He was the first man she dated. She was with him the week we arrived.'

'This McCauley chap,' Fulton said, 'could he have been the one she had an argument with?'

Adler pursed her lips and thought for a moment. 'He was the first one she dated, so yes,' she said. 'We'd only been here a couple of weeks when she spoke about it.'

Hathaway took the second photograph and handed it to Baird. 'And this man,' he said. 'Could this be the Danny or Dave that you mentioned?'

She took the print, glanced at it, and nodded. 'Yes. I only saw him the once, but yes. They drove in his car and parked as I approached the dorm. They got out and stood talking for a bit. Clare smiled and waved as I passed.'

'When was this?' Hathaway asked.

Baird furrowed her brow. 'Let's see… last Tuesday. No, wait… Wednesday. Yes, definitely. I was on my way back from the campus library. I always go on Wednesday evenings, it's their late opening night.'

'Do you happen to remember what time?'

'Around eight, I think. The librarian was getting ready to close as I left.'

Hathaway nodded, took out another print, and said to Baird, 'I think this photograph shows you and Ms Adler together with two other girls – can you tell me who they are?'

Baird took the print and studied it for a few moments. 'Yes, I can. It was taken by Clare a couple of weeks ago. We're in the campus café. The girls sitting to my right are Sandrine Cudlipp and Rebecca Ryan.'

'The two friends you mentioned earlier?' Fulton asked.

'Yes,' Baird said. 'Like I said, they're in the dorm next to ours.'

'And in this,' Hathaway said, handing her another print, 'Clare is seated next to you and Ms Adler?'

Baird took a quick look and nodded. 'Yes. Sandrine took that one.'

'Clare was interested in photography?' Fulton asked.

Adler pointed to a camera on a shelf near the door. 'Yes,' she said. 'That's hers. It's a Canon AE-1 SLR, which takes film. She told me she completed a photography course in Moray College in Nairn, where she is from. I, too, studied photography, in Bamberg. Soon after I arrived in Edinburgh I accompanied her to Holyrood Park just before dusk one evening. We took pictures of the castle.' She stifled a sob, adding, 'She let me borrow her camera.'

'This morning,' Fulton said, 'Clare was out early. That was a habit?'

'Uh-huh,' Baird said. 'She liked to keep fit and went for a run most days. Sofia and me didn't share her interest, we were barely awake when she left.'

'How long was she normally gone for?' Fulton asked.

'Depends,' Adler said. 'Usually forty minutes. But if she saw something and wanted to take a picture, it could be longer.'

Baird nodded agreement. 'She posted her images to Instagram. Had quite a following.' She paused, then added, 'We began to worry around eight-thirty. She'd been gone for more than an hour and a half by then.'

'Yes,' Adler said. 'We usually have breakfast together before heading to university. It was only when we came back from the café the janitor told us there had been an accident at the Crags. We worried it might be Clare.' She took a tissue from inside her sleeve, wiped her eyes, and shook her head. 'But I did not know then she was dead…'

Fulton nodded sympathetically. 'I know it's not pleasant, girls, and we appreciate your cooperation,' he said. 'Just another couple of questions and we'll be on our way. First, your friends next door, you know if they're still here?'

Baird shook her head. 'We were slightly late in getting back from breakfast, by which time they would have left to attend lectures. As Sofia said, we were intercepted by the janitor, who broke the news about someone found injured. Only afterwards were we told by the dorm supervisor it was Clare.'

'I see,' Fulton said. 'Okay, that just leaves the lads — Fraser McCauley and the other chap.' He glanced at Baird. 'You told us their dorms are on the ground floor. You don't happen to know which numbers?'

'No, sorry,' she replied. 'But the dorm supervisor's flat is the first you come to as you enter at the ground floor. She should be able to tell you.'

Chapter Four

After Fulton and Hathaway departed, Knox studied transcripts of DI Niall Paterson's interviews then he and DS McCann left the station and headed for Kaimes Green.

As he steered his Passat onto North Bridge, Knox glanced at McCann and grinned. 'So, Arlene,' he said. 'You've been hiding your light under a bushel.'

McCann gave him a mystified look. 'Sorry, boss,' she said. 'I'm not following you.'

'The narcotics course DCS Steele told us about.'

'Oh, that,' McCann replied, shaking her head. 'Three days spent taking in a bunch of statistics.'

'Statistics?'

'Uh-huh. Like how many Class A drugs by weight were seized by Police Scotland last year.'

'Really?' Knox said. 'Do tell.'

'One hundred and eighteen kilos of heroin. Seventy-five kilos of cocaine. More than twenty-five thousand ecstasy tablets.'

Knox shook his head in disbelief.

'Want me to continue?' McCann said.

'Please.'

'Average yearly death rate due to drug use in Scotland is around 0.2 per 1,000 people, apparently. And it's higher in urban areas'

'Jesus – anything else?'

'Uh-huh,' McCann said, warming to the subject. 'How to recognise signs of substance abuse, particularly heroin. Users' eyes tend to be affected with myosis; opposite of dilation – pupils contract to a pinpoint. Other markers, sometimes not so obvious, are needle marks – inside of the elbow, back of the hand, behind the knees, between the toes. The veins of long-term users can collapse.'

'Gross,' Knox said. 'I recall reading somewhere that at the height of the coke craze in 1980s America, the US treasury tested their banknotes and found most had traces of cocaine.'

'Yeah, I remember seeing that, too.'

'Wouldn't happen here, though.'

'You reckon?'

Knox gave wry smile. 'U-huh. All our notes are made of bloody plastic.'

McCann chuckled. 'Aye, you're right.'

They drove without speaking for a short while afterwards, then McCann broke the silence. 'By the way, boss, I forgot to tell you how sad I was to hear about Yvonne.'

Yvonne Mason was the officer McCann had replaced on Gayfield Square's murder inquiry team. Her predecessor, who Knox was engaged to and planned to marry, had been stabbed to death by a crazed rapist six weeks earlier.

Knox's face clouded. 'Thanks.'

'I'm sorry I couldn't attend the funeral. I was on a murder inquiry in Ullapool.'

'I heard, Arlene. Appreciated the flowers, by the way.'

'Least I could do,' McCann said. 'I heard your son came over?'

'Yeah, Jamie and his wife, Anne.'

'Your granddaughter, Lily?'

'They left her with Susan.'

Susan was Knox's ex-wife, who had moved to Moreton Bay near Brisbane in Australia after she and Knox divorced in 2006. Their son Jamie gained a degree in dentistry and he, his wife and daughter had joined Susan in 2014.

'The guy – sorry, boss, let me know if I'm hitting a nerve – he's still on remand?'

'Tate?' Knox almost spat out the killer's name. 'Likely his case won't be heard till July of next year.'

The pair lapsed into silence again, and arrived at Kaimes Green a few minutes later.

'The crescent, wasn't it?' McCann asked.

Knox gestured ahead and flicked on his indicator. 'Yeah, third opening on the right once we enter Kaimes Green Drive.' He tapped the dashboard. 'My satnav's on the blink; had to check Google Maps before we left the station.'

Knox came to a stop moments later outside 9 Kaimes Green Crescent, one of a row of terraced houses with cream-harled walls that predominated in the area. Knox indicated the house, which lay beyond a neatly trimmed hedge and small garden. 'Sandy Purvis,' he said. 'The ex-bus driver who witnessed Norman Smeaton's murder. Thigh grazed by a 9mm Parabellum round from a Glock 19 automatic pistol. Luckily, only a flesh wound, for which he received three stiches at A&E and was allowed home. In his statement to Paterson he says he didn't get a particularly good look at Smeaton's killer.'

'Steele thinks it's worth speaking to him again?' McCann said.

Knox shrugged. 'Uh-huh. Though Paterson's interview appears thorough enough. The same goes for the one he conducted with Smeaton's widow.'

'She's at 23?'

Knox nodded. 'Further along the crescent.'

The detectives exited the car and were almost at the gate when the door opened and a man in his late sixties appeared. He had a set of keys in his hand, and held a black Labrador on a leash. 'Yes?' he said.

'Mr Sandy Purvis?' Knox asked.

'Yes.'

Knox and McCann held out their warrant cards. 'Detective Inspector Knox and Detective Sergeant McCann,' Knox said. 'We're here to speak to you about the death of Mr Smeaton last Thursday.'

Purvis gave Knox a disgruntled look. 'I spoke to one of your detectives on Friday,' he said. 'Told him everything then.'

'I'm aware of that, sir,' Knox replied. 'It was in case we missed something.'

Purvis shook his head. 'Don't see how that could be. Your sidekick was here for over an hour.'

Knox motioned towards his car. 'We could come back later if it's inconvenient. You were going out?'

'Aye, I was.' Purvis tut-tutted and pushed open the door. 'It was only to give the dog a walk, get a few things. It can wait.' He beckoned, adding, 'You'd better come in.'

The detectives entered and followed him into the living room, where he pointed to a settee. 'Sit yourselves down,' he said, then slipped the dog's leash and nodded to the hallway. 'I'd better take Sadie into the back garden. I think she's in need of a pee. Going on twelve, her bladder's not what it was.' He shook his head. 'Glad of her company, though. It's three years since my wife passed.'

Purvis left the room and reappeared moments later, taking an armchair opposite the detectives. 'Okay, what do you want to know?'

'I apologise in advance if I cover some of the stuff DI Paterson – that's the officer who spoke to you on Friday – asked about,' Knox said. 'Like I said, it's in case we've missed something.'

'Aye, okay.'

Knox took out his notebook and consulted his notes. 'You left home at approximately 3.15pm to take your dog for a walk–'

'Aye, the same way I go every day, towards the local shops,' Purvis interrupted. 'Sadie was with me.'

'And you were passing 23 Kaimes Green Crescent when you heard a car at your back?'

'Couldn't help but hear it,' Purvis said. 'The bugger's tyres were squealing as he turned in from Kaimes Green Drive. Drove along the crescent like it was the Nürburgring.' Purvis paused. 'Nürburgring – that's what you call it, the racetrack in Germany?'

'That's right, yes,' Knox agreed.

'Thought it was,' Purvis said, and went on, 'When I get near Smeaton's house I see him in his garden, cutting grass. I glance around and spot the car – a dark blue Beamer – approaching at speed. The driver brakes hard, tyres burning rubber. Comes to a stop level with the garden, then I hear popping sounds – you know, like firecrackers?'

'Yes, go on.'

'Well, next there's a high-pitched pinging sound, like something hitting metal. I feel a sharp pain in my left thigh; my leg gives way, and I fall to the ground. I hear another series of popping noises, and the BMW accelerates away. By now the pain is excruciating, and I lie facing the pavement. Almost simultaneously I hear a woman screaming.' Purvis shook his head. 'I discovered later it was Smeaton's wife, lying over the body of her dead husband.'

'You told DI Paterson you didn't see who was in the car?'

'It happened quickly,' Purvis said. 'I remember seeing a driver, but no passenger. As I told your mate, I reckon he must've had the nearside window rolled down. Likely he leaned over to shoot – I'm pretty positive I didn't hear the car doors open or close.'

'You're sure the only occupant was the driver, yet you didn't see what he looked like?'

Purvis nodded. 'I've thought about that since I spoke to Peterson.'

'Paterson,' Knox corrected.

'Aye, Paterson.' Purvis said. 'I think I'm right about him leaning over before he started shooting. There would only have been a fraction of a second between him stopping the car and taking aim.' Purvis ran a thumb over his chin. 'I've replayed the scene in my mind a few times since Thursday, though, trying to recall more. If I had to make a guess, I'd say he was dark-haired and wearing black.'

'Thanks, that might prove helpful,' Knox said. 'One other thing – Smeaton's house isn't far from yours. How long would you say it takes you to walk there?'

'Only two or three minutes. Why?'

'Do you remember passing anyone before the incident. Someone who might have been using a mobile phone?'

Purvis thought for a moment. 'Hmm,' he said. 'Now that you mention it, there was a young chap walking ahead of me as I left the house… and, yes, I recall he was talking on a phone as he passed Smeaton's place. He was almost out of view at the other end of the crescent when I heard the BMW.'

'This man,' Knox said, 'what did he look like?'

Purvis shook his head. 'I dunno, only saw him from the back. Late teens, early twenties. Wearing jeans, I think, and one of those bomber jackets. Oh, aye, and he wore a Yankee-style hat, a bright red one.'

'A baseball cap?' Knox asked.

'Aye,' Purvis agreed. He shifted in his armchair, winced and then murmured, 'Ooh!'

McCann gestured towards his leg. 'Still painful?'

'Uh-huh,' Purvis said. 'Certain ways I move. Not as bad as it was, though. I'm still taking painkillers, get the stitches out on Thursday. Doctors at the infirmary tell me I'm lucky. A few millimetres to the left and it would have shattered the thigh bone.'

'The bullet ricocheted?' McCann said.

Purvis nodded. 'Off one of the mower's metal handles, which accounts for the pinging sound I heard. Inspector Paterson told me one of your people found the slug in the pavement, a few feet from where I fell.'

Knox closed his notebook, stood up, and McCann followed his lead. 'Okay, Mr Purvis, we won't take up any more of your time. I very much appreciate your talking to us.'

'Sorry if I was sharp when you arrived,' Purvis said. 'It's just that the whole business came as a bit of a shock — not only my being shot, but journalists knocking at my door at all hours wanting an interview. I had no idea the lad was in the drugs racket. This has always been a nice area.'

'Smeaton had been here long?' Knox asked.

'Four or five years, I think. He and his wife seemed such a respectable couple.'

Chapter Five

'Poor old soul,' McCann said when they were back in the car. 'Takes a quiet walk to the shops, gets shot, then is plagued by journalists.'

'And coppers,' Knox said.

'Aye,' McCann acknowledged wryly. 'And coppers.'

'I think our interview was worthwhile, though,' Knox said. 'Everything he told Paterson, and something else.'

'The fella with the phone?'

'Uh-huh. Smeaton's killer had to make sure his target was vulnerable. Someone carried out a recce and discovered he cut his lawn regularly. The guy with the bomber jacket walked by to make sure.'

'Then rang whoever was in the Beamer, and Smeaton's fate was sealed.'

'Exactly.'

'The suspect, Wallace,' McCann said, 'we know what he looks like?'

Knox nodded. 'Yeah, I had a quick glance at Paterson's file. Thirty-seven years old. Medium build, dark hair — certainly fits the description. No luck with CCTV, though. Paterson reports there are cameras on the two main access routes into the area — one outside a bank in Liberton

Gardens, the other at a garage in Lasswade Road. Recordings were checked for the period between 10am and 4pm on Thursday. No sightings of a dark-blue BMW.'

'So we've drawn a blank on that one,' McCann said. 'What now?'

Knox pointed along the street. 'We drive a bit further down,' he said. 'Have a chat with Smeaton's wife.'

* * *

Glassel House's supervisor was a prim, oval-faced woman in her late fifties, who opened the door to her flat and peered at the detectives over a pair of horn-rimmed spectacles. 'Yes,' she said haughtily. 'Can I help you?'

'Detective Sergeant Fulton and Detective Constable Hathaway,' Fulton replied, showing his warrant card. 'We're investigating the death of one of your students, a Ms Clare Tomkins.'

'Oh, I see,' the woman said, softening a little.

'We're in the process of interviewing people she knew,' Fulton continued. 'We've already spoken to Ms Adler and Ms Baird. They tell us Ms Tomkins was friendly with a couple of lads who reside on this floor. The girls said you may able to help – you're the block supervisor?'

'Yes, I am,' the woman replied. 'Ms Rhona Adams. Do you happen to know the young men's names?'

'Only one,' Hathaway said. 'Fraser McCauley. The other we're not sure of. Ms Tomkins' friends think his Christian name is Danny or Dave.' Hathaway took a print from the envelope and handed it to her. 'He's the man in this picture.'

Adams studied the picture for a moment. 'That's David Martin,' she said. 'I know that for sure because I know him well, his mother's a close friend.'

'He's in one of the rooms on this floor?' Fulton asked.

'Yes,' Adams replied. 'Dormitory G7. The other young man you spoke of, Fraser McCauley, is resident next door, Dorm G9.' She pointed along the passageway. 'Other end of the corridor.' She glanced at her watch. 'But I don't think you'll find them there now. Both attend lectures at Edinburgh University Medical School. If you come back around four, however…'

Fulton nodded. 'Yes, probably a good idea. There's a couple of Ms Tomkins' girlfriends we've to see, a Ms Cudlipp and Ms Ryan.'

'Ah, the young ladies in 4c?' Adams said. 'Yes, Ms Ryan should be back then, but I'm afraid Ms Cudlipp left yesterday morning. Had to return to Leicester – a family bereavement. Don't think she'll be back till later in the week.'

As the detectives left Glassel House and headed to the car. Fulton glanced at his watch. 'Almost two-thirty, Mark,' he said. 'Don't know about you, but I'm famished. There's a wee caff at the foot of East Preston Street. Let's get some lunch, kill a bit of time, come back and do the other interviews around four – what do you say?'

Hathaway patted his stomach. 'Good idea, Sarge. Left in a bit of a rush this morning, just managed a couple slices of toast.'

Fulton nodded. 'Okay, son. That's it settled.'

* * *

Knox's press on the bell was answered by a drawn-faced woman in her late twenties, who opened the door a fraction. 'I've said all I'm going to say, given all the interviews I'm going to give,' she said sharply, then began to close it again.

'We're not the press, Mrs Smeaton,' Knox said, showing her his warrant card. 'I'm Detective Inspector Knox and this is my colleague Detective Sergeant McCann.'

Smeaton kept the door ajar and eyed the pair contemptuously. 'I talked to the police on Thursday,' she said. 'Cops were all over the place after they took Norrie away.'

'I know,' Knox said. 'You spoke to Detective Inspector Paterson.'

'Aye, that was the guy. He was here for hours, went over everything.'

'I understand, Mrs Smeaton,' Knox said. 'Thing is, sometimes after a traumatic event, it can take a day or two to remember things clearly. After-effects of shock.' Knox nodded to a hallway beyond her shoulder. 'Would you mind if we came in? I promise we won't keep you longer than we have to.'

Smeaton studied Knox for a long moment, then shrugged her shoulders and waved them inside. 'Aye,' she said with resignation. 'Not for long, mind. I've my wee girl to pick up. My sister Laura's been looking after her since Norrie was…'

As her voice trailed off, she reached into the pocket of her slacks and took out a tissue. She began dabbing her eyes.

McCann asked, 'Your daughter, what's her name and how old is she?'

Smeaton sniffed. 'Sarah. Going on four, still at nursery.'

The detectives entered and Knox indicated a door on his left. 'Okay if we talk in the living room – that's in here?'

'Aye, sorry,' Smeaton said. 'The banquette's in the corner by the window. Take a seat.'

Knox and McCann went to a corner unit facing an elaborate oak bar, around which several stools were positioned. Smeaton slid behind the counter, took a glass, and pressed it under the optic of an upended vodka bottle.

'A bit early, I know,' she said, 'but I'm having a drink. My nerves are shot to hell.' She paused after pouring and motioned to the detectives. 'You'd like something?'

'Not for me, thanks,' Knox said.

McCann shook her head. 'No, I'm fine.'

Smeaton carried her vodka to the corner of the banquette and sat facing them. 'I'm not much of a drinker,' she said. 'Usually, that is.' She sniffed again and shook her head. 'But this is so bloody unreal.' She wiped tears from her eyes and went on, 'Norrie was only thirty-one. The bastards didn't have to kill him.'

'Do you know why someone would want to do that?' Knox asked.

'As I told your mate on Thursday, I knew what Norrie was into.' She waved to her surroundings. 'But, contrary to what you might think, we didn't get any of this from drugs; the furniture, a nice house with fully paid-up mortgage, new car – all legit. My husband was on the rigs for seven years and made very good money.'

She shook her head, and continued, 'He was on shore leave in Aberdeen a few months back. One of his so-called pals offered him a line, and within weeks he was hooked. He wasn't a heavy user, but still had a dependency. His work suffered as a result and his boss let him go.

'Give him his due, Norrie didn't sell the car, furniture, or hock any belongings to fund his habit. No, he found someone who inveigled him into dealing in exchange for drugs and a top-up of what dole money he got. I was pissed at him, of course, and threatened to leave. Pleaded with him to think of the bairn. He promised he'd change, but never did.'

'Was he ever pulled for dealing?' Knox asked.

'By your lot?' she said. 'No, I wish he had been. A spell inside might have brought him to his senses.'

'The person who supplied the drugs, you know who he is?'

Smeaton shook her head. 'No, he never told me and we never discussed it. He said it was better if I didn't know.'

'Your husband would've communicated with his supplier?'

'Aye,' Smeaton said. 'Via his mobile. When it rang he went to the kitchen or into the garden.'

'He never discussed those conversations?' McCann asked.

'No,' she said. 'And I didn't want to know.'

'But your husband crossed swords with someone,' Knox said. 'You've no idea who?'

Smeaton put down her glass on a nearby coffee table and reached for a tissue. 'I'm not stupid, Inspector,' she said, dabbing her eyes. 'I know what he was doing was dangerous. Someone had it in for him, that's obvious. He just made a habit of never speaking about it. It was his way of protecting me.'

'And no one ever called at the house?' Knox asked.

'No. Whoever he saw, he saw in the car.'

'Did your husband keep drugs at home?'

'No, never. Anything to do with drugs was done out of the house. He made sure it stayed like that.'

'You didn't notice any change in his behaviour in the days leading up to the shooting?' McCann asked.

Smeaton shook her head. 'No,' she said. 'If anything was going on, I wasn't aware of it.'

'Okay,' Knox said. 'Last Thursday. At approximately 3.15pm your husband was in the garden when a dark blue BMW pulled up outside. Where were you when the shooting began?'

'In the kitchen, putting clothes into the tumble dyer. Norrie was in the garden and I could hear the sound of the mower. Suddenly, I heard a sequence of popping noises, like a car backfiring – but over and over; six, seven times. The kitchen's at the side of the house, so I couldn't see out front. But all at once I'd a horrible feeling. I can't explain it, but I knew instinctively something was wrong. I rushed to the door and saw a car driving off and Norrie collapsed on the lawn. I ran to where he lay and turned him over, but...' Smeaton's voice trailed off and she stifled a sob.

'You didn't see who was in the car?' Knox asked.

'No. I can't even remember what happened next. It was like I was in some sort of trance. Someone must've phoned for an ambulance and Norrie was taken to the infirmary.' She began to weep. 'I found out later he was pronounced dead on arrival. It's been five days and I've still not been able to see him or make funeral arrangements. Paterson said they won't release his body till they've finished doing tests.'

'My colleague and I will be stopping off at St Leonards Police Station on our way back. DI Paterson's based there. We'll have a word with him and find out when the pathologists are likely to release him. I'll ring you this afternoon,' Knox said.

'Would you?' she said. 'It'd make me feel so much better.'

Knox and McCann took their leave then and Smeaton escorted them out.

* * *

'DI Paterson's temporary office is room 41, Inspector Knox,' the desk sergeant at St Leonards was saying. Knox and McCann arrived back from Kaimes shortly after 1pm and had driven directly to the station.

'Give him a ring, will you, Charlie?' Knox said, then gesturing to McCann, added, 'Arlene and I are going for lunch. I'd like to speak to him afterwards.'

The detectives made their way to the canteen, where Knox surveyed a menu tacked to a pillar next to the hotplate. 'I recommend the steak pie, Arlene,' he said, grinning. 'If previous experience is anything to go by.'

'Not for me, boss,' McCann said. 'I don't eat meat, remember?'

'Aye, sorry,' Knox said. 'You did mention it.' He nodded to the hotplate. 'The haddock's not bad either.'

Chapter Six

The canteen was almost empty and Knox and McCann were finishing their meal when a man entered and approached their table. He was square-jawed and heavily built, with sandy hair combed over a thinning pate. 'You're Knox?' he said.

'Aye,' Knox said, extending his hand. 'DI Paterson?'

Paterson gave Knox's hand a perfunctory shake, then pulled a chair from an adjoining table and sat alongside, ignoring McCann.

'I'll be honest up front, Knox,' Paterson said. 'Can't fathom why DCS Steele had to bring you in. Me and my lads were cooperating with his plans to bring down McMahon and Wallace. I was up to speed with the undercover guys Skinner and Hammond, too. Now the DCS has pulled my lads and asked me to work with you.'

Knox glanced at McCann and back at Paterson, then motioned towards his companion. 'I don't believe you've been introduced to my DS,' he said. 'DI Paterson, meet Arlene McCann.'

Paterson gave her a look of indifference, and nodded. 'Aye, hello, hen.' Then, to Knox he said, 'So, what do you say?'

'About what?'

'What I was saying; my being stood down from the Macintosh interview. It was unnecessary.'

'What did DCS Steele say?'

'I'm not sure what you mean.'

'The reason for your being asked not to do the interview,' Knox said.

Paterson grunted. 'He said you'd a history with Macintosh; some kind of affinity.' He shook his head. 'Don't see how a copper could have a rapport with a bawbag like that.'

Knox pushed his plate to one side and laid his hands on the table. 'In 1997,' he said, 'Macintosh was stopped for speeding and a bag of cocaine was found in his possession. I interviewed and charged him, and his brief later persuaded the judge that the coke was for personal use. Macintosh was given a suspended sentence and fined £500.

'Apparently he thought it a good idea to try and ingratiate himself afterwards. He sent a letter to the chief constable praising my, ahem, politeness. Maybe he thought it would deflect suspicion from what he subsequently got up to.' Knox gave Paterson a pointed look and, with a hint of sarcasm, added, 'I wasn't aware of any "rapport" at the time.'

'And Steele thinks Macintosh might respond better to you?' Paterson said. 'I don't see the logic in that.'

'Frankly, neither do I,' Knox said. 'But he's the one with the scrambled egg on his cap. If you're unhappy I suggest you take it up with him.'

Paterson grunted, was silent for a moment, then said, 'The sergeant at the front desk said you wanted to ask me something?'

'Aye,' Knox said. 'Arlene and I are just back from Kaimes Green Crescent. We spoke to Sandy Purvis and Lisa Smeaton. Everything they said pretty much agrees with your report.'

'Uh-huh,' Paterson said. 'I believe I was fairly thorough.'

'There was *one* thing, though.'

Paterson scowled. 'What was that?'

'Sandy Purvis. He saw a young guy – late teens, early twenties – walking in front as he left his house and headed along the crescent.'

'Aye?'

'Purvis saw him talking on a mobile as he passed Smeaton's house; seconds later the BMW appeared.'

'The driver was tipped off?'

'The killer had to be sure of his target,' McCann said. 'He had someone watch Smeaton's movements.'

Paterson glanced at McCann in surprise, as if he'd forgotten she was there. He turned back to Knox. 'Purvis never said anything to me.'

'Probably skipped his mind,' Knox said. 'He was still traumatised when you spoke to him.'

'Aye, probably,' Paterson replied. 'So, one of Wallace's cohorts made sure Smeaton was in the open.' He paused, then added, 'You told me you spoke to his wife, too? She'd nothing to add?'

'No,' Knox agreed. 'I asked if Smeaton kept drugs in the house. She said no – your searches confirmed that?'

'Aye. We'd a dog unit in. A Spaniel sniffed upstairs and down, didn't find a trace. As you say, his wife swore he never kept gear in the house, so maybe he had a lockup somewhere.

'Hard to believe she'd no knowledge of his business, though,' Paterson added, shifting in his seat. 'You saw the fancy bar, 32-inch Sony tv, new furniture? And what about his Golf GTi, impounded for forensics? Top of the range, worth thirty-two grand. She knew all right. They were making plenty.'

'Lisa claims he earned good money on the rigs,' McCann said. 'She told us he got into drugs only a few months ago.'

'Aye, and the band played,' Paterson said, spittle flecking his lips. 'No, she gave me that story, too. I asked if she could produce receipts. They were in the house, she said, just couldn't remember where exactly. No, she knows a damn sight more than she's telling.'

'Your report said a mobile was found on him?' Knox said.

'Aye, a pay-as-you-go. Only two numbers on it: a landline in Gracemount that turned out to be a phone box. The other a top-up mobile. We checked; it'd been burned.'

'So,' Knox said, 'his connection with McMahon, there's no proof?'

Paterson shook his head. 'No, no proof, but he was Smeaton's supplier all right. All business is done via mobile phones – the aforementioned pay-as-you-go variety. I spoke to DS Skinner, the undercover guy who has McMahon's ear. He tells me McMahon has four or five guys fencing gear for him. They're mobile, carry top-up phones. Orders come in, they meet the user and, voila, the transaction takes place. Smeaton was one of those guys.'

'Why was there only one mobile number on Smeaton's phone – he must have got calls?'

'McMahon has them delete numbers and texts after every transaction.'

'Then how did he contact McMahon?' Knox asked. 'Either to get drugs or pay for them?'

'Skinner told me McMahon texts a code word to his guys' mobiles. Each indicates a prearranged time and place. A supermarket car park at 7.30pm, for example. They complete the exchange and are gone in minutes.'

'Okay, Smeaton's murder,' Knox said. 'DCS Steele said he would have supplied someone outside McMahon's territory?'

'Oxgangs,' Paterson said. 'Wallace's patch. Skinner says McMahon's been trying to muscle in there for months. We think Smeaton was spotted – a brand-new Golf GTi in that part of town? Would've stuck out like a sore thumb. Wallace got to hear and ordered the hit.'

'Surely Smeaton was aware of the danger – he'd have known Oxgangs was off limits?'

'Likely he had no choice. Do McMahon's bidding, or else. No more dough; no more drugs.'

'And McMahon knew how Wallace might react?' Knox asked. 'Smeaton was expendable?'

'Uh-huh. He was testing the waters. And Wallace's reply was "You're out of your depth."'

Knox said nothing, and Paterson added, 'Macintosh, you've seen him yet?'

'No, not yet,' Knox said.

'You've thought how you'll steer him into thinking McMahon and Wallace are getting ready to jump ship?'

Knox studied Paterson for a long moment, then said, 'Anything in that direction has to appear plausible – you agree?'

'Of course.'

'We have to make Macintosh believe we've sussed his connection with McMahon?'

'No question.'

'I was thinking,' Knox said, 'that you might talk to McMahon, unsettle him a little.'

Paterson was taken aback. 'Me?'

'Uh-huh,' Knox said. 'You said Smeaton had a pay-as-you-go phone?'

'Aye?'

'What if a call was made to his mobile, later traced to McMahon?'

'McMahon wouldn't swallow that,' Paterson protested. 'He'd know he didn't make such a call.'

'You said he sends texts?'

'I told you, he has them wiped.'

'But McMahon *could've* rung Smeaton?' Knox said. 'It's smoke and mirrors, remember: the aim is to make Macintosh believe we've had comms people checking

McMahon's calls, including one to Macintosh himself.' He paused. 'Which allows me to be convincing about his guys' double-dealing, the reason for my visit.'

'And how are you going to do that?'

'I tell him we traced another of McMahon's calls,' Knox said. 'To a high-profile dealer in Strathclyde.'

Chapter Seven

Fulton's press on the doorbell at dormitory G7 was answered by a freckle-faced man dressed in T-shirt and jeans.

'David Martin?' he asked.

'No, I'm his room-mate, Clive Parker,' the man replied. 'Davie's not back yet.'

Fulton consulted his watch. 'I was told he returns around four. It's quarter past now.'

The man nodded. 'Yes, normally he would be. But on Tuesdays he stops off at Tesco. Will I say who called?'

Fulton shook his head. 'No, it's okay. We'll come back.'

'It's about Clare, isn't it?' Parker said. 'You're police?'

'Yes,' Fulton replied.

'I only heard when I returned from uni,' Parker said. 'I don't think Davie knows yet, either.' He shook his head. 'He'll be devastated; they were seeing each other.'

'Not to worry, son,' Fulton said. 'We can speak to him later.'

Parker gave a nod of understanding, closed the door, and the pair walked the short distance to the adjoining dormitory. As they approached, the door to G9 opened and a young man began to exit. He had a large canvas holdall in one hand and began to close the door with the other.

Hathaway immediately recognised him from his photo. McCauley looked a bit shorter in real life, he thought, and a little less ruddy-faced.

He stared at the detectives in surprise. 'You want to see me?' he asked.

'You're Fraser McCauley?' Fulton asked.

'Yes.'

'Detective Sergeant Fulton and Detective Constable Hathaway,' Fulton said. 'We're investigating the death of a young student in Holyrood Park this morning, a Ms Clare Tomkins. I believe you knew her?'

'I did, yes.'

Fulton indicated the bag. 'We caught you at a bad time?'

'Oh, this?' McCauley said, shaking his head. 'No, only dirty washing. I was headed to the launderette.'

'I see,' Fulton said. 'You mind if we speak a moment?'

McCauley re-entered the dormitory, threw the holdall on the floor, and opened the door wide. 'No, not at all,' he said. 'Come in.'

The detectives went inside and McCauley motioned to a couple of chairs. 'Please,' he said.

Fulton and Hathaway took a seat, then McCauley went on, 'I take it you've spoken to Clare's girlfriends?'

'We have, yes.'

'They told you Clare and I were seeing each other?'

'Yes,' Fulton agreed.

'We dated a few times at the start of term,' McCauley said.

'You were still seeing her?' Fulton asked.

'No.' McCauley shrugged. 'She lost interest.'

'The two of you had an argument?'

McCauley's jaw clenched. 'Who told you that?'

'Just answer the question, please,' Fulton said.

'The affair lasted a couple of weeks,' McCauley said. 'Then suddenly she refused to see me again. I didn't understand why, I thought things were okay between us. I asked if she was seeing someone else, but she denied it. Said it was all getting a bit intense, she needed some breathing space.'

'You had a row?'

'Yeah.'

'When did this happen?' Fulton asked.

'I don't know what you mean.'

'When you and Ms Tomkins argued. What date?'

'Not long after the start of term, I think. I can't be sure of the exact date.'

'Okay,' Fulton said. 'What happened then?'

'We argued back and forth a bit. She accused me of being clingy, then stormed off. I discovered later the reason she wanted to finish. She *had* met someone else.'

'She told you that?' Hathaway said.

'She didn't have to. A few days afterwards I saw her with him – Davie Martin, a guy in the next dorm.'

McCauley fell silent for a few moments, then his jaw dropped. 'Wait a minute!' he exclaimed. 'It *wasn't* an accident, was it? Clare didn't fall from those cliffs, did she? That's why you're here… you think I killed her.'

'We're conducting an investigation into the cause of Ms Tomkins' death, sir,' Fulton said. 'We're not ascribing guilt to anyone at the moment.'

McCauley gave Fulton a searching look. 'But she *was* murdered?'

Fulton shook his head. 'Sorry, I'm not in a position to confirm that at the moment.'

McCauley snorted. 'I think you just did.'

Fulton gave him a thin smile. 'Then you won't be surprised if we have to ask where you were at seven-thirty this morning.'

'I was here, getting ready for breakfast.'

'Someone shares this dormitory with you?' Hathaway asked, nodding to two other beds, on which duvets and pillows lay neatly folded.

'No,' McCauley replied. 'There was a short intake of students this term. I've got the place to myself.' He shook his head. 'Look, I was in the café when it opened at eight. I couldn't have risen, washed and shaved, and made my way over there if I'd been running in Holyrood Park, now could I?'

'You're in the habit of doing that, Mr McCauley?' Fulton asked.

'Doing what?'

'Running in Holyrood Park.'

McCauley shrugged. 'Sometimes.'

'Did you ever accompany Ms Tomkins on a run?'

'No,' McCauley replied. 'I only found out she was in the habit of running after we split. When I jog it's in the afternoon, not mornings as Clare did.'

'So you were never in Holyrood Park with her?' Hathaway asked.

'No.'

Hathaway took a photograph from the envelope and placed it on a table beside McCauley, who looked increasingly perturbed as he inspected the image.

'That was taken shortly after I met her,' he said. 'We walked to the foot of Arthur's Seat and back. I wasn't lying – you can see we aren't wearing jogging gear.' He tapped the picture. 'I'd forgotten about it, we were only there for half an hour.'

Fulton stood and walked towards the door. 'Okay, Mr McCauley,' he said. 'I think that'll do for now. You're aware we may have to speak to you again?'

'I am,' McCauley replied. 'And I'm sorry about Clare,' he added. 'But her death had nothing to do with me.'

* * *

'You're the police officers who spoke to the girls in 2c earlier?' the young woman was saying. Fulton and Hathaway had reached the second-floor corridor when they heard her voice behind them. Martin had still not returned when they left McCauley, and they'd decided to revisit the second floor instead.

'Sorry,' she added. 'Perhaps I should introduce myself. I'm Rebecca Ryan.'

Fulton turned and saw the girl was around twenty, similar in age to the young women they'd spoken to earlier. She looked taller, though, and had raven hair and high cheekbones.

'Yes, we are,' he agreed. 'Ms Adams advised us you'd be back around now.'

Ryan's face clouded. 'Yes, I spoke to her on the way here. She told me about Clare. What a horrible thing to have happened. Rhona said you'd already seen Fiona and Sofia – I take it you want to talk to me, too?'

'If it's convenient,' Fulton said. 'We wouldn't keep you long.'

Ryan shook her head. 'No, it's okay. I had nothing planned.' She caught up with the detectives and nodded towards dormitory 4c. 'I'm just along here.'

They arrived at the dorm and Ryan waved them inside, indicating a couple of chairs. As Fulton and Hathaway took a seat, Ryan went to a corner unit and nodded to a cafetiere. 'I was just going to make coffee,' she said. 'Would you like one?'

Fulton shook his head. 'No, but thanks for asking,' he said. 'We're fine.'

Ryan switched on the coffee maker, which soon came to the boil. She filled a mug, added milk and sugar, and sat opposite the detectives. 'So,' she said. 'What would you like to ask?'

'The girls at 2c told us you were all friends?' Fulton said.

'Yes,' she said, then gave a wistful smile. 'We called ourselves the Famous Five.' She motioned to a bed opposite. 'Sandrine's not here at the moment. She had to return home, a family bereavement.'

'Yes,' Fulton said. 'Ms Adams told us.'

Hathaway glanced at a third bed, positioned nearer the door. 'So it's just you and Ms Cudlipp sharing this dorm?'

Ryan took a sip of coffee. 'You're wondering about the spare bed?' she replied. 'Very occasionally we put up foreign students arriving in Edinburgh on their way to other universities in Scotland. St Andrews, say, or Aberdeen. They'll arrive too late to make an onward connection, and on those occasions temporary accommodation will be arranged with Ms Adams for them to bunk here. They usually stay only one night, though.'

'Your friends told us Ms Tomkins was a keen runner,' Fulton said. 'Most days she was in the habit of rising early and doing a circuit around the Crags. They told us they didn't share her interest. Did either you or Ms Cudlipp?'

Ryan shook her head emphatically. 'No. I cycle to Heriot-Watt college and back, but that's all. Sandrine's a keen swimmer, but I don't think she jogs.'

Fulton nodded. 'When was the last time you saw Ms Tomkins?'

'Sunday night, I think.' Ryan paused for a moment. 'Yes, Sunday night, around eight o'clock. She and I had a couple of lattes in the café. David Martin came in soon afterwards and sat with us. The three of us talked for a while, then I left them and came back here.'

'And when Clare left for her jog this morning,' Hathaway said, 'you didn't see her?'

'At seven-thirty? No, I was sleeping.' Ryan smiled. 'I never stir until the alarm goes.'

Chapter Eight

'That DI Paterson's a rude bugger, don't you think, boss?'
McCann was saying. 'I can understand why DCS Steele
wanted you to interview Macintosh.' She and Knox were
approaching traffic lights on Lanark Road, which had just
turned to red.

Knox changed down, braked gently, and brought his
car to a stop. 'His manner with Lisa Smeaton you mean,
asking for receipts when her man's just been murdered?'

'Aye, damned callous.' She shook her head. 'Bit of a
chauvinist, too. He pretty much ignored me.'

Knox nodded. 'Yes, I'd to pull him up on that.'

'Yeah, boss, I noticed. Thanks.' She paused then added,
'When is he seeing McMahon?'

Knox glanced at his watch. 'Nearly three now,' he said.
'I told him to time his arrival at McMahon's place for 3.15.
Same time we drop in on Macintosh. We've officers in
unmarked cars checking both locations. They'll contact
Paterson; confirm both targets are at home.'

'And if either one isn't?'

'We'll abort. Try again tomorrow.'

The traffic lights changed back to green and, as Knox
moved off, an amplified ringing came from the speakers.

Knox pressed the dash-mounted iPhone's *accept* button. 'Knox,' he said.

'It's Paterson,' a voice said. 'We've a go. Targets in place at both locations.' A pause, then, 'I'm two minutes from McMahon's place in Captain's Road. You at Gillespie Road yet?'

'Almost,' Knox said.

'Okay. We see both parties at three-fifteen?'

'Affirmative.'

'Okay. Speak to you later.'

As Paterson terminated the call, Knox turned left into Gillespie Road, and McCann said, 'What number?'

'Sixty-nine,' Knox replied. 'Halfway down on the left.'

A few moments later Knox pulled in, stopped, and pointed to a large white-painted villa, which was sheltered by trees and reached by a gravel driveway. 'We'll park here,' Knox said. 'Best to walk in – draw less attention to ourselves.'

He and McCann exited and covered thirty or so yards to an arched porte-cochère, at the right-hand side of which a dark grey Bentley Mulsanne was parked.

McCann nodded in its direction. 'Fruits of his labours, eh, boss?' she said quietly.

'Aye,' Knox replied. 'Courtesy of a barrel of rotten apples.'

He thumbed a ceramic bell push set in a square of polished brass, and moments later the door was opened by a man in his mid-thirties. He was tall and muscular, with the kind of physique Knox guessed was gained more by steroids than lifting weights.

He reacted to Knox and McCann's presence with only one word: 'Yeah?'

'Is Mr Macintosh at home?' Knox asked.

'Who wants to know?'

The detectives took out their warrant cards and Knox said, 'Detective Inspector Knox and Detective Sergeant McCann.'

'Who is it, Roddy?' The voice came from the hallway, and the moment he heard it, the man stood to one side. 'Cops, Mr Mac,' he said deferentially.

'Police?' came the reply, and a slight man with thinning hair appeared.

Macintosh had changed little in the twenty-odd years since he saw him last, Knox thought. He was around sixty now, but had the same wiry appearance.

'Why, Mr Knox,' he said. 'How are you, sir?'

'You remember me?' Knox said.

'How could I forget? You were the only one who showed me any kindness at the time of that unpleasantness at Newington.' He glanced from Knox to McCann and added, 'But surely this isn't an official visit?'

Knox dipped his head in acknowledgement. 'Isn't a social call, I'm afraid.'

Macintosh nodded to his companion. 'It's okay, Roddy, you can go.' As the man took his leave, he turned back to Knox. 'I'm sorry to hear that.' He waved to the hallway and added, 'But won't you and your colleague come in?'

The detectives followed him along a short corridor. He opened a door on the left, entered, and the detectives followed. Knox looked around the room, which appeared to be a study. Bookshelves lined a wall on one side and a substantial rosewood desk was positioned in front of a large picture window. Macintosh gestured to a couple of leather-upholstered chairs in front of the desk. 'Sit yourselves down,' he said.

As Knox and McCann complied, Macintosh walked to the other side and settled into a large armchair, which looked part of the same suite of furniture.

'Sorry about Roddy,' he said. 'He doesn't do pleasantries very well.' Macintosh pressed a buzzer on the desk, and added, 'I was just about to have afternoon tea — you'll take some with me?'

'No, thanks,' Knox replied. 'We had a late lunch.'

There was a light knock on the door and a middle-aged woman entered the room. 'Mr Mac?' she said.

'Pot of tea and the usual, Isa,' Macintosh said.

The woman motioned to the detectives. 'And your guests, sir?'

Macintosh gave Knox a querying look. 'You're sure you won't have anything?'

'No, honestly,' he said. 'We're fine.'

Macintosh nodded. 'Just for me, Isa, thanks.'

The woman left the room.

'Okay, Mr Knox,' Macintosh said. 'Perhaps we better get to the reason for your visit.'

'It concerns a man called Norman Smeaton,' Knox replied. 'He was shot dead outside his home at Kaimes Green Crescent last Thursday.'

Macintosh leaned forward on his desk. 'Yes, a nasty business,' he said. 'But the only thing I know about it is what was reported in the *Evening News*. Drug-related, wasn't it?'

'There's evidence for that, yes,' Knox agreed. 'Mr Smeaton was a low-level dealer pushing drugs for a man called McMahon who, we've reason to believe, is behind the distribution of Class A narcotics in the south-east of the city. McMahon's supplier has another distributor, responsible for south-west Edinburgh, whose name is Wallace.

'We're sure McMahon and Wallace's supplier has an agreement that neither man will encroach on the other's territory. We think this agreement was breached. Apparently, Smeaton – McMahon's man – strayed into his competitor's patch and concluded one or more deals. Smeaton's death was sanctioned by Wallace in retaliation.'

Macintosh shook his head. 'As I said, a nasty business, but I don't understand what it has to do with me. As you know, my own involvement with drugs ended many years ago. And, as my solicitor proved at the time, the quantity of cocaine I had on me was for personal use.' He paused, then added, 'Surely you don't think I'd anything to do with this?'

'I don't know, Mr Macintosh,' Knox said. 'But a mobile phone was found in Mr Smeaton's possession. We checked and found one of the calls received was from McMahon. In the course of our investigation we had a network engineer check all calls made by McMahon in the last fourteen days. One of those calls was traced to your landline.'

There was a light tap at the door again and the woman called Isa came in, laid a tray on Macintosh's desk, and departed. Macintosh poured tea into a china cup, added milk and stirred in sugar, and swallowed a mouthful.

Macintosh replaced the cup in its saucer. 'I don't know how to answer that, Mr Knox,' he said. 'But, as I say, if you think I'm involved, you're steering the wrong course. Mr McMahon must've dialled my number by mistake.

'You may be aware that over the last twenty-one years I've built up a very successful retail fruit business,' he continued. 'I've three very busy shops in the better areas of town. Last year my net turnover was almost three million pounds.' Macintosh pointed to a filing cabinet across from the desk. 'My accounts are available for your inspection at any time. All my business is legal and above board.'

Knox nodded. 'I appreciate that, Mr Macintosh. But on the question of a wrong number; no, I'm afraid it doesn't work like that. You see the call connected for a full three minutes.'

'But that's impossible,' Macintosh said. He stared at Knox for a few seconds, then his brow furrowed. 'Wait – the call in question. What time was it made?'

Knox glanced at McCann, who checked a notebook on her lap. 'Last Friday,' she replied. '11.15am.'

'I think I know what's happened,' Macintosh said. 'We've been getting a lot of spam calls lately – the usual thing; outfits purporting to be Amazon Prime, British Telecom and the like. My chauffeur Roddy, the lad who came to the door – helps around the house when he's not driving me somewhere – also answers the phone.

'Last Friday I found the hall telephone off the hook. When I asked, he told me he'd been so annoyed listening to automated voices that he'd taken to leaving the handset off the cradle for a few minutes. On that occasion, however, he forgot to put it back. It's been a misdial, Mr Knox, which Roddy's taken for a spam call. It must have been off the hook for three minutes before I replaced it.'

'I see,' Knox said. 'That would certainly account for it.'

Macintosh remained silent for a long moment, then said, 'These mobile network technicians, Mr Knox, they're able to do that now? Trace when and to whom calls are made?'

'Yes,' Knox said. 'The technology's very sophisticated. They were able to tell us, for example, that later last Friday – at 4.25pm to be exact, McMahon made a call to one of the biggest drug dealers in the west of Scotland.'

'Really?'

'Uh-huh,' Knox said. 'We know on that occasion the call lasted for 11 minutes and 44 seconds. We suspect the dealer – who's located in Cambuslang – is likely to be McMahon and Wallace's supplier.'

Macintosh shook his head, but his face betrayed no emotion. 'Amazing,' he said, then shrugged his shoulders. 'Well, I trust that I've managed to satisfy you that I know neither man?'

Knox and McCann stood and made ready to leave. 'Well, we'll have to take another look at the network records to make sure the call was indeed a misdial,' he said, 'but I'd say, yes, we're satisfied.'

Macintosh emitted an audible sigh, and smiled. 'Good,' he said. His expression became serious again, and he added, 'Oh, by the way, Mr Knox, I was terribly sorry about your fiancée.'

'Pardon me?' Knox said, not sure he'd heard correctly.

'I know it's still likely to be painful,' Macintosh said. 'So forgive me for bringing it up. I was talking about Yvonne Mason, the young officer who was murdered a month or so back. You *were* engaged to be married?'

'Yes,' Knox said. 'We were.'

'I read about it at the time,' Macintosh said. 'Derek Tate, the man who killed her, he's still on remand in Saughton?'

'Yes.'

'I thought so,' Macintosh said. 'You know, I met him a couple of years back. I know George Turnbull, the property agent he worked for. Bought my third shop from him, the one in Stockbridge. It was Tate who dropped off the deeds.'

Macintosh fell silent for a long moment, and added, 'Contrary to what you might think, Mr Knox, he won't have an easy time inside. They're not liked, you know, men who kill women. The fact she was a police officer won't make any difference.' He shook his head. 'Tate had better watch his back.'

Chapter Nine

'You think he swallowed it, boss?' McCann was asking. Several minutes had passed since they took their leave of Macintosh, and she and Knox were driving back into town.

'All that business about us having traced McMahon's calls?' Knox replied.

'Yes.'

'Well, I'd say we were lucky his guy Roddy's been answering a number of spam calls lately,' Knox said. 'And just happened to receive one around the time I gave his boss.'

'Macintosh's still likely to check, though?'

Knox nodded. 'Nothing surer. And McMahon'll swear blind he never made such a call. Which is true, of course.'

'The Cambuslang cartel gambit,' McCann said. 'He tried to hide it, but I think it came as a shock.'

'Which is what Steele wanted. Ruffle his feathers; get him to react.'

'So what happens now?'

Knox shrugged. 'That's up to Steele, Paterson and the narcotics unit. No doubt they'll stake him out, await his next move.'

'Then we're free to concentrate on the Tomkins murder?'

'Yes, which reminds me,' Knox said. He placed his iPhone on the dash-mounted holder and pressed *call*. 'I've to give Turley a ring.'

A few moments later a middle-aged woman's voice answered, 'Cowgate Mortuary, how may I help you?'

'Afternoon, Maisie,' Knox said. 'Is Alex there?'

'Afternoon, Inspector Knox,' the woman said. 'Yes, he is… hold on a moment. I'll put you through.'

A few seconds later they heard pathologist's voice. 'Jack?'

'Hi, Alex. The Tomkins girl – were you able to complete the PM?'

Turley cleared his throat. 'Aye, which confirmed my initial findings. As I told you this morning: death due to major head trauma. The fall caused serious spinal fractures, too, both cervical and thoracic. One thing I wasn't able to discern earlier, though, were pre-fall injuries.'

'You found something?'

'Aye, I did,' Turley said. 'Significant contusions of the pectoralis and trapezius muscles, upper chest.'

Knox shook his head in bafflement. 'Sorry?'

'She was beaten about the chest and shoulders,' Turley said. 'Before she fell.'

'So it's homicide?'

'Little doubt, Jack. Little doubt.'

'Thanks, Alex, that's pretty helpful.'

'All in a day's work.'

'By the way,' Knox said, 'there was one other thing.'

'Go on.'

'The shooting last Thursday at Kaimes. The pathologists at Gartcosh are conducting a post-mortem on the deceased, a Norman Smeaton. Thing is, I was asked to help with the investigation and interviewed his wife. I promised I'd try to discover when her husband's body might be released.'

'You'd like me to check?'

'If you wouldn't mind, Alex, please.'

'No problem, Jack. I know the woman in charge, Professor Lorna Wright. Leave it with me. I'll give her a ring, get back to you.'

'Appreciate it, thanks.'

'Okay. Speak to you later.'

No sooner had Knox ended the call than the speakers reverberated with an incoming call. Knox answered it and said, 'DI Knox?'

'Aye, Knox. Paterson here. Just finished up at Captain's Road. Thought you'd like to know the outcome of my visit to McMahon?'

'Uh-huh,' Knox said. 'Go ahead.'

'I had to soft-pedal a bit. Told him were acting on an anonymous tip-off, which resulted in us having engineers trace his mobile phone calls. He was adamant he hadn't rung Smeaton. Demanded a printout of the calls, said he'd take it up with his solicitor if need be.'

'M-hmm,' Knox said. 'So, not a great deal of joy?'

'No, but at least I kept him talking a good ten minutes. Followed up by asking if he'd ever met Smeaton, to which the reply, naturally, was negative. I finished by having him give an account of his movements on Thursday and Friday.'

'You didn't mention Macintosh?'

'No, I thought I'd leave that part of the ensnarement to you.' A pause. 'How did it go, by the way?'

Knox gave him a précis of his interview, ending with Macintosh's reaction to McMahon's call to Cambuslang.

'You think he bought it?' Paterson asked.

'Pretty confident, yes,' Knox said. 'I take it the next move will be to keep an eye on Macintosh?'

'Yeah,' Paterson agreed. 'I'll give DCS Steele an immediate report on our interviews. No doubt he'll take it from there.'

* * *

'It's definitely murder, then?' Fulton was saying. Knox and McCann had arrived back at Gayfield Square, where they and the other two members of the team were discussing the Tomkins case.

'Yes,' Knox confirmed. 'And it happened under cover of fog so she wouldn't have seen her attacker until the last minute.' He paused for a moment, then added, 'How did it go at the Pollock Halls?'

Fulton went over the interviews he and Hathaway had conducted with Tomkins' room-mates and Rebecca Ryan and Fraser McCauley, and added, 'The other chap she'd been seeing, David Martin, hadn't arrived back when we returned later in the afternoon, so we'd to leave him till last.'

'How did he seem?' Knox asked.

'Distraught,' Hathaway replied. 'He didn't learn of her death until he arrived back at Glassel House.'

'Aye,' Fulton agreed. 'Took it hard. He and Tomkins were at the cinema last night, which was the last time he saw her. Incidentally, he was in his dorm around the time Ms Tomkins died. Clive Parker, the guy who shares with him, was able to substantiate that.'

'McCauley,' Knox said, 'you're satisfied with his story?'

'Well he admitted the row had been heated,' Fulton said. 'He hadn't been expecting her to throw him over for Martin.'

'When did the argument take place?' Knox asked.

'They began seeing each other soon after the start of term,' Hathaway said. 'He told us it lasted for two weeks. He reckons late September.'

'A long time to nurse his wrath,' McCann said.

Knox nodded. 'My thoughts exactly. Tomkins would've been seeing Martin for two or three weeks. Why wait until now?'

Knox remained silent for a long moment, then addressed Fulton, 'What's your thinking, Bill?'

Fulton shook his head. 'No gut feeling either way, boss. McCauley has the dorm to himself, so no corroboration there. Told us he was at the campus café when it opened at 8am, but that proves nothing. He could easily have made the Crags and back again. Admitted to being a regular jogger, too, but maintains he confines his running to the afternoons.'

'So, no real alibi?'

'No, boss.'

'I caught him out on one thing,' Hathaway said.

'Oh?'

'Aye. He told us they were never in the park together, however, a photograph from Tomkins' iPhone shows both of them there shortly after they met.' He shrugged. 'He claimed he forgot when I tackled him about it.'

The phone on Knox's desk rang at that moment and he picked up the handset. 'Knox?'

'Davie Roker, sergeant on the front desk, boss. Got a call on the line. A young woman, sounds muffled. Claims she's got information on the Clare Tomkins murder.'

'Okay, Davie, thanks. Put her through.' He reached for the speaker switch and turned to the others. 'You may want to listen to this.'

He turned on the speaker and said, 'Hello, Detective Inspector Knox?'

The desk sergeant had been correct about the voice. The young woman appeared to have covered the mouthpiece with a cloth or a tissue.

'Hi,' she said. 'You're the officer in charge of the Clare Tomkins case?'

'I am, yes.'

'Before we start, I want to remain anonymous. Is that understood?'

'Okay,' Knox said.

'All I'm prepared to say is that I'm a student, resident at Glassel House.'

'Go on.'

'I visited a friend on Monday evening who was having a party to celebrate her birthday. I had few drinks and stayed later than I planned. She invited me to sleep over, and I accepted. I'd to get back to my dorm early this morning, though, as I had to pick up textbooks and notes before going on to university.' A pause. 'Hello – you still there?'

'I'm listening,' Knox said.

'I thought I'd been cut off.'

'Uh-huh,' Knox said. 'What time did you get back to the Pollock Halls?'

'I was just about to say. I arrived at Holyrood Park Road a few minutes after seven. I was approaching the entrance to the campus and saw Clare Tomkins leave and head towards the park. I knew it was her because she usually goes jogging at that time.' There was a long silence, then, 'Sorry, I was putting more coins in the box.'

'Okay,' Knox said. 'Carry on.'

'Seconds later a man in running gear came out of the gate and headed in the same direction. I recognised him straightaway: it was Fraser McCauley. I thought nothing more about it until I overheard someone in the café say detectives had spoken to him this afternoon. Then heard rumours Clare had been murdered. I think he was her killer.'

'What makes you say that?'

'Because they were an item once. She stopped seeing him and began dating someone else. When she called it off, he hit her – hard. She'd a black eye for the better part of a week.'

'How do you know all this?'

'Sorry, I've already said enough.'

'Wait,' Knox said. 'We'd like to–'

There was a distinct *click* and the line went dead. Knox took the handset from the speaker unit, pressed a button, and was connected to the switchboard.

'Sergeant Roker.'

'Davie,' Knox said. 'The woman rang off. The call was made from a public call box. Find out where it's located and get back to me, will you?'

'Boss.'

Knox turned to the others. 'We'll have another word with McCauley.' Then to Fulton, 'Have uniform pick him up, Bill. Tell them to look for his running shoes, too. Have them bag them and bring them in. I'll ask Murray if there's a chance of matching anything on them with soil at the top of the Crags.'

As Fulton moved towards his desk the telephone rang again.

'Davie?' Knox said.

'Newington Road at the corner of West Preston Street, boss,' Roker said. 'I checked if we'd anything in the area. Nearest car was at Causewayside. They had a look, but she'd gone.'

Chapter Ten

'This feud between you and Shug Wallace has gone far enough, don't you think, Gus?' Macintosh was saying. He was talking to McMahon from a telephone box in Colinton Village, a short drive from his home in Gillespie Road. The Bentley Mulsanne was parked in a cul-de-sac a short distance away. His chauffeur, Roddy, sat patiently at the wheel, reading a copy of *The Sun*.

'Then it's him you should be speaking to, Tosh, not me,' McMahon replied.

'I have,' Macintosh said. 'Tells me Smeaton supplied a couple of his regulars in Oxgangs. Even gave them a bloody discount.'

'Wallace should take a leaf out of my book. Try being a bit more competitive.'

'You're not serious, Gus, surely? You're poaching in his territory.'

'Getting a bit of my own back,' McMahon said. 'His guys have been seen in Buckstone – my patch.'

'Buckstone?' Macintosh said disbelievingly. Buckstone was an upper-middle-class area in the south of the city where detached villas sold for £500,000 and upwards.

'Aye, Buckstone,' McMahon said. 'The rich are partial to some of Colombia's finest, too. Though usually it's sniffed up their noses, not needled into their veins.'

Macintosh heard pips at that moment and pressed a pound into the slot. 'I'm calling from a phone box, Gus. It's not long since I had a visit from the cops. Smeaton's murder's stirred up a hornet's nest. They know his connection to you – they're keeping tabs on our calls, for Christ's sake.'

'Crap,' McMahon said. 'I had the cops here, too, a guy from the narc squad, name of Paterson. Fact is, I never called Smeaton. It's an attempt to create panic.'

'Well, it's bloody working. They know you called me at 11.15 last Friday morning.'

'Who said that?'

'I told you, a couple of detectives interviewed me less than an hour ago. A DI Knox and a DS McCann. Knox told me they had a record of your calls.'

'Well, it's bullshit. I never called you and Knox knows it. Like I said, they're trying it on.'

'You think so?'

'The cops know Wallace murdered Smeaton, but can't prove it. They suspect he worked for me, but can't prove that, either. They've nothing to go on. What's more, it's going to stay that way.'

'So you and Wallace – you'll bury the hatchet?'

'I'll bury it in his fucking head if he tries anything else,' McMahon said. A short pause. 'You told me you spoke to him?'

'I knew nothing about Buckstone then. You're sure he was supplying your clients?'

'One hundred per cent.'

'Okay,' Macintosh said. 'I'll have another word with him.'

'Right, and make sure he listens. Else next time it'll be him taking a bullet.' A short silence, then, 'Oh – and, Tosh?'

'Aye?'

'I thought you'd a couple of disposable mobiles – burners?'

'I have.'

'You don't have to worry about using them. Mobile technology's good, but not that good. If you use a burner and get rid of it afterwards, you're safe. There's no way they can trace you. Like the mobile you're calling me on now. I'll dump it when we finish this call. I'll snail mail you the number of the new one, like I did last time.'

'Okay,' Macintosh said, and added, 'So Knox was lying about the calls you made last Friday?'

'Put it this way, Tosh. What he told you was every bit as real as rocking horse shit.'

Macintosh ended the call, walked back to the Bentley and got into the back seat.

Roddy put down his paper. 'Everything okay, Mr Mac?' he asked.

His boss shook his head. 'Not quite. The two guys you were telling me about. They'd be up for a bit of contract work?'

'Absolutely sure of it.'

'They drive, have their own transport?'

'Sammy Reid has a Corsa, Bert Allison a Mondeo.'

Macintosh nodded. 'Get in touch, I have a job for them.'

'Will do, Mr Mac.'

'And, Roddy?'

'Mr Mac?'

'That lad you know in Saughton, Pete Gifford. He's contactable?'

'Uh-huh. He has access to a mobile. Able to use it after lights out.'

'Good,' Macintosh said. 'I'd like to talk to him about an inmate, a guy called Tate.'

* * *

Sammy Reid was waiting for a snooker table in the Chesser Arms when his mobile rang. He took the phone from his pocket, eyed the screen cautiously, then his companion said, 'Anyone you know?'

Reid gave his mate a hard stare. 'Dunno till I answer, do I?'

The man shrugged and his attention drifted back to the table, where a youth in a checked shirt had pocketed his second red.

Reid keyed *accept*. 'Hello?'

'Hi, Sammy,' a voice answered. 'Roddy here. How're you doing?'

Reid gave a nervous laugh. 'Fine, Roddy, thanks.'

'Get the envelope?'

'Aye, Roddy, thanks for dropping it off. The fifty was much appreciated.'

'Least I could do for an old cell-mate. How're you managing?'

'Not bad.'

'Your second week out?'

'Aye, still to report to Torphichen Place, my local cop shop. Wednesdays.'

'They're not hassling you?'

'No, Roddy, just routine.'

'Right. By the way, you've still got your Corsa?'

'I have, Roddy, yeah.'

'It's running okay? Taxed and insured?'

'Of course.'

'Where are you? Sounds noisy at your end.'

'I'm in the Chesser Arms. Waiting for a snooker game.'

'Right.' Roddy paused for a moment, then added, 'Listen. You're still friendly with Allison?'

'Aye, Bert. He's here with me.'

Bert Allison turned at the mention of his name, then Reid covered the mouthpiece and whispered, 'Roddy Moran.'

Allison nodded, then his attention was drawn back to the table, where the man in the checked shirt had pocketed a succession of balls and was cueing the black. He nudged Reid and said, 'Looks like we'll be on in a minute.'

'Sammy?' Roddy said.

'Aye, Roddy. Still here.'

'Bert, doesn't he run a Mondeo?'

'Aye.'

'It's in okay shape?'

'Aye, Roddy. Quite a nice set of wheels.'

'Good. The two of you meet me at Merlin in Morningside at seven tonight. Got a wee job. Worth a grand each. Sound okay?'

Reid gave a wide grin. 'Sounds absolutely fine, Roddy.'

* * *

'I told you all you wanted to know when you interviewed me earlier,' McCauley was saying. The student had been brought to Gayfield Square and sat across a table from Knox and Fulton in Interview Room 2. A NEAL taping device had been switched on and was recording the conversation.

'New information has come to hand we need to check out,' Knox replied. 'Which is why you're being reinterviewed. I should emphasise you're not under arrest. However, there are one or two things we need to clarify.'

McCauley shook his head. 'I don't understand,' he said. 'What new information?'

'Before we get to that,' Knox said. 'You made a statement to DS Fulton that you were in the habit of jogging in Holyrood Park, is that correct?'

'Yes.'

'But only in the afternoon? Never in the morning?'

'Yes.'

'You also told DS Fulton that you were at the campus café in time for it opening this morning. You didn't go for a run beforehand?'

McCauley studied Knox for a long moment. 'Somebody said I did? This is the "new information" you're talking about?'

'To be frank, Mr McCauley, it is. We were told you left the Holyrood Park entrance to the Pollock Halls at just after seven this morning, and that Ms Tomkins left only moments before you.'

McCauley's face reddened in anger. 'That's a load of bloody nonsense,' he said. 'Who is this person?'

'Someone who prefers to remain anonymous,' Knox said.

McCauley shook his head. 'What – a malicious phone call?' he said. 'One of the students trying to make trouble?'

'Why should someone want to do that?' Knox asked.

McCauley shrugged his shoulders, but said nothing.

'This afternoon you told DS Fulton that you and Ms Tomkins argued? She said she didn't want to see you again?'

'We exchanged words and, yes, it got a bit heated. I told your colleague that.'

'You struck her?' Knox asked.

McCauley gave him a look of surprise. 'Struck her?' he said. 'This person said that?'

'Please, Mr McCauley, just answer the question.'

'I never touched her. Anyone who says anything to the contrary is lying.'

'Clare had a bruise around her eye for almost a week after the two of you broke up,' Fulton said. 'How do you explain that?'

'Another lie,' McCauley said. 'Or if she had such a bruise it had nothing to do with me.'

'One final thing,' Knox said. 'When you jog in the afternoons, which part of the park do you use?'

'I run via Duddingston Low Road to Duddingston Loch and return the same way.'

'You never use the Radical Road or Hunter's Bog?'

'You're talking about the route Clare used, aren't you? You still suspect I followed her?'

Knox held McCauley's gaze, but said nothing.

'No,' McCauley said. 'I've not been in that part of the park for ages.'

Knox nodded. 'Okay, Mr McCauley, you'll be aware the officers who brought you here took a pair of trainers belonging to you?'

'Yes,' he replied. 'I'd to show them where they were: next to a radiator in the corridor outside the dorm, where I left them yesterday.'

'Uh-huh,' Knox said. 'And did the officer explain why we were taking them?'

McCauley shrugged. 'To do some kind of test?'

'Yes,' Knox agreed. 'One of our forensics officers has confirmed that the cliffs where Ms Tomkins fell has a soil containing fine Carboniferous basalt. If you've been in the area lately, your trainers will have picked it up – you understand?'

McCauley gave Knox a defiant look. 'I'm not lying, Inspector,' he said. 'I told you the truth. I didn't see Clare this morning. And I was nowhere near her when she died.'

Chapter Eleven

Rebecca Ryan had just made herself a coffee and was checking a textbook when she was suddenly conscious of someone else in the room. She looked up and, seeing her friend, said, 'Sorry, Louise. Didn't see you there.'

Louise gave her a haughty look. 'You quite often don't.'

Ryan smiled. 'Come now, you know that's not true.' She tapped the textbook, and added, 'I was concentrating, that's all.'

Louise harrumphed. 'You had a visit from the police yesterday?'

'I did,' Ryan admitted. 'They were asking about Clare.'

'What did you tell them?'

'That I didn't see her. I told them I was asleep when she left to go jogging.'

'You told them about seeing her with David?'

'In the café? Yes, I did.'

'But you didn't mention me?'

'No, not a word.'

'Good,' Louise said. 'I'd better remain your little secret, don't you think?'

* * *

'You didn't tell me about Buckstone,' Macintosh was saying. He had just finished breakfast and was using one of his disposable mobiles to ring Wallace.

'What about it?' Wallace replied.

'Gus tells me you're supplying his punters in the area. We agreed Comiston Road was the demarcation line. Your territory is everything to the west, his to the east.'

'The punter in question,' Wallace said, 'is mine. He moved house from Swanston in my patch to Buckstone, a matter of a mile or so. What was I supposed to do – ring McMahon and hand him over?'

'You could've advised him, yes. No need to go killing one of his pushers and putting the entire operation at risk.'

'Smeaton's murder wasn't meant to happen. I intended a warning. The guy who got the job was told to shoot Smeaton's windows in, not kill him. He panicked when he saw McMahon's pusher in the garden, thought he might identify him. Lost his head and shot the place up.'

'Okay,' Macintosh said. 'Regarding your punter from Swanston, I'll speak to Gus again and see if we can come to an agreement.' A pause. 'You're sure he's the only one you're supplying there?'

'Only the one, aye,' Wallace replied. 'What about Oxgangs?'

'Again, I'm sure we can come to an arrangement to make sure neither of you infringes on the other's territory,' Macintosh replied. 'You'll give me your word in the meantime there'll be no further trouble?'

'If he stays on his side of the line, no problem. If he doesn't…'

'Okay, Shug. Leave it with me.'

Macintosh ended the call and handed the mobile to his chauffeur, who was in the study with him. 'Get rid of that on your way to the village, will you, Roddy?' he said.

'No problem, Mr Mac,' Roddy replied, then gave Macintosh an earnest look. 'Everything okay?'

Macintosh shook his head. 'Like a pair of squabbling bairns, they are.' A pause, then, 'That other business, you took care of it?'

'Reid and Allison?' Roddy said. 'Aye, spoke to them last night.'

'They're up to the job?'

'I'm sure they'll be fine, Mr Mac. Reid was my cell-mate for a while. An okay guy; ex-marine, turned security guard. Worked for a while in London, did some surveillance training.'

'And Allison?'

'Reid vouches for him, he seems capable enough.'

'You briefed them?'

'Yeah. They'll stakeout Wallace and McMahon. Tail them discreetly and keep an eye on their movements. Switch around every day to minimise suspicion. Report back to me.'

'They know to take registration numbers?'

'Yeah, all details will be logged.'

'Good,' Macintosh said. 'McMahon said Knox was bullshitting about the calls on Friday, but I'm not sure. I think he and Wallace are up to something.'

* * *

'The Tomkins girl, Jack,' Warburton was saying, 'any progress?' The DCI was behind the desk in his office and Knox was seated opposite.

Knox brought his boss up to date on McCauley's statement at Glassel House, the anonymous telephone call, and the student's reinterview at the station the previous evening.

'I told him about the caller's allegations, of course,' Knox said. 'And that we'd be conducting forensic tests on his trainers.'

'He didn't appear fazed?'

'No, sir. Quite the opposite; adamant that the caller's insinuations were false.'

Warburton drummed his fingers on the desk. 'You think the tests will come back negative?'

'I'd be surprised if he'd anything to do with Tomkins' murder, to be honest, sir.'

The phone on Warburton's desk rang at that moment and Warburton picked up. 'Yes?' he said.

Warburton's tone was immediately deferential. 'Oh, yes, sir. He's with me now.' He covered the mouthpiece and added, 'It's DCS Steele. He wants to speak to you.'

Knox took the receiver and said, 'DI Knox.'

'Morning, Knox,' Steele replied. 'Paterson reported your interview with Macintosh, and his own with McMahon. Good work. I think our moves are beginning to have the desired effect.'

'Macintosh has made contact with his source?' Knox asked.

'No, not yet. But I think he's beginning to have doubts about his lieutenants' loyalty. Our surveillance team keep a round-the-clock watch on his house, and last night Rodney Moran, his chauffeur-cum-factotum, was followed to The Merlin Public House in Morningside.'

'Macintosh was with him?'

'No,' Steele said. 'On his own, used his own car, a Renault Megane. He met two men there, a Sammy Reid and Bert Allison. Both have form. Allison completed six months of a nine-month sentence in Peterhead for housebreaking. Reid was released from Saughton ten days ago. Another recidivist, burglary in his case.' Steele paused. 'Reid has an interesting history. Joined the Royal Marines at twenty, served six years. Applied for the Special Boat Squadron during that time, but was turned down. Later worked with Group 4 Security, underwent close protection training. We know, too, that his pal Allison completed an advanced driver course.'

'What's Reid's connection with Moran?' Knox asked.

'They were cell-mates in Saughton. Moran was previously a nightclub bouncer. Served three months for GBH.' Another pause. 'Able to join the dots yet?'

'Macintosh's hiring them to keep tabs on McMahon and Wallace?' Knox said.

'Precisely. I've been in touch with Skinner and Hammond. Told them to keep an eye out for Reid and Allison's cars, a Vauxhall Corsa and a Ford Mondeo. Sightings of either will confirm our suspicions.'

'When they report your undercover officer's meetings, Macintosh is likely to act?'

'We hope so, DS Skinner is meeting McMahon today. His car's wired, and we're ready to reel him in. Hammond's doing the same with Wallace.'

'But you need Macintosh to contact his source before you make your move?'

'Yes,' Steele said. 'We think it'll take another persuasive nudge to do it. Which is why I'd like you to see him again.'

Knox was surprised, but said nothing.

'Less than an hour ago,' Steele continued, 'Moran left Macintosh's house at 69 Gillespie Road and drove to Colinton Village, as he's done every morning since we've had the place under surveillance. He visits a wee shop there; buys papers, rolls, etcetera and makes his way back. This morning my men followed his Megane to the village and watched him park. But instead of going straight to the shop as he normally does, he backtracked – walked to where a bridge spans the river. You know the spot I mean?'

'Yes,' Knox said. 'Where Gillespie Road crosses the Water of Leith.'

'Exactly,' Steele agreed. 'He walked back, stopped, and had a quick look around. Satisfied no one was watching, he took a paper poke from his pocket and threw it over the handrail. My men waited till he'd done his shopping, then went down to the river and retrieved the package. It contained a pay-as-you-go mobile phone. Unregistered, of course.'

'You checked with the service operator?'

'We did. It was last used to call a mobile in Broomhall Grove. The call terminated at 8.37am.'

'Macintosh used it to call Wallace?'

'Yes.'

'But I don't understand, sir,' Knox said. 'If I talk to Macintosh, won't it have the opposite effect – make him wary about contacting his source?'

'No, the call is unimportant.'

Knox gave an involuntary shake of the head. 'I don't follow.'

'It's less complicated than it sounds, Knox,' Steele replied. 'I want you to speak to Macintosh again. Only this time it's about what Wallace is up to.' There was a long silence, then Steele went on, 'The purpose of your visit is to let him know we found the mobile and suspect it was his. The idea is to give him cognisance of a call Wallace made afterwards. The recipient – surprise, surprise – is the same person McMahon called on Friday in Cambuslang.'

'But if he swallows that,' Knox said, 'he might be wary of contacting his source – particularly if he thinks his calls are being monitored.'

'I disagree,' Steele replied. 'I'm sure he'll do exactly what he did after you interviewed him yesterday – go to a phone box.'

'He used a payphone?'

'Yes. Moran drove him to Colinton Village in the Bentley. Parked in Spylaw Street while his boss went to a coin box across the street. We think he was ringing McMahon to check on your story.'

'Then there's all the more reason to doubt Macintosh will fall for that a second time,' Knox protested. 'Paterson said McMahon saw through the bluff, threatened to call his lawyer.'

'I've a feeling he mightn't place a great deal of weight on anything McMahon tells him,' Steele said. 'In any event, as I said at the outset, the prize is well worth the stake. What do you say, Knox – you'll talk to him?'

'Okay, sir,' Knox said resignedly. 'I'll give it a shot.'

'Good man.'

* * *

The Asda car park at Brunstane was busy, the area nearest the supermarket moderately full, so DS Keith Skinner drove to a verge at the bottom where there were still vacant spaces. He reversed his Volkswagen Polo into a marked box, making sure he left room for parking on either side.

Skinner, alias Andy Nolan, then checked his watch: 10.48am. He had ten minutes in hand, as he'd arranged to meet McMahon at 11.00. McMahon favoured big supermarkets, as there were always shoppers coming and going, less chance of anyone taking notice of two men in a car.

The undercover officer reached under the car's dashboard and gave the rocker switch a reassuring check. It was out of sight, wired to a recording device located beneath the rear seats.

He glanced up in time to see McMahon's silver-grey Audi A6 glide into the entrance. As it began to head in his direction, Skinner activated the switch.

McMahon drove nose-first into a space on his left, exited the car, opened the Polo's nearside door, and slid into the passenger seat.

'Morning, Andy,' he said. 'Everything okay?'

'Aye,' Skinner replied. 'You?'

McMahon shrugged. 'Still taking fallout from the actions of that bastard Wallace,' he said. 'Narc squad paid me a visit yesterday, a guy called Paterson.'

'Giving you grief?'

'Nothing I can't handle. The arsehole tried to bluff me. Said an engineer checked calls to Smeaton's phone. I'm supposed to have rung him. A load of bullshit, and I told him so.'

'How'd it finish up?'

'Promised I'd get my brief onto it, didn't I? Then he changed tack, asked me to account for my movements on Friday, and buggered off.'

'You hadn't phoned the guy?'

'Course not.' McMahon touched the side of his nose. 'I make it a rule. Easy to get caught if you've too much contact with the pushers.'

Skinner nodded sympathetically. 'Yeah, know what you mean.'

McMahon looked Skinner straight in the eye. 'So, you spoke to your bosses? What'd they say?'

'Aye, happy with ten thousand a kilo less than you pay Macintosh.'

'Yeah? And you mentioned how much I shift every week? No problems with supply?'

'I told you, Gus,' Skinner replied. 'We're a big outfit. Cover the whole of Strathclyde.' A pause. 'Macintosh won't give you problems?'

'When I leave him, you mean?'

'Aye.'

McMahon made a face. 'Naw,' he said. 'The cops paid him a visit too, yesterday. Same spiel they gave me. Told him they'd monitored calls to his place, had a record of one made by me. More bullshit. He appears to have believed it, though.'

'Aye?'

'Aye. They told him I'd called. It spooked him: he rang me from a public phone box.'

Skinner shook his head, feigning incredulity, but said nothing.

'You might find this hard to believe,' McMahon continued, 'but Wallace and me started together. Dealt with an outfit in Newcastle. Drove up and down the A1, shifting fifty kilos and upwards a week before we found Macintosh.'

'Who put you onto him?'

'An old guy, Stuart Grant, made most of his money in the 1990s. Got out of the game and retired to Spain.'

'But losing you,' Skinner said, 'will mean a fair drop in income. Macintosh is bound to be pissed.'

'Aye, no doubt,' he said. 'But that's as far as it'll go. He's not the type to try anything. Anyway, he still has Wallace.' McMahon shrugged and added, 'No, I don't expect trouble. He'll accept it and move on.'

'Hmm,' Skinner said. 'What about his source? Any backlash there?'

'Nah, I don't think so. In two years Macintosh's never talked about where he gets his gear. I've been curious, of course; just never felt the need to pursue it. If I'd to guess, I'd say it's someone from your neck of the woods.'

'The west?' Skinner said. 'I doubt it. There are only two big outfits, and we're one of them. What makes you say that?'

McMahon shrugged. 'Nothing specific,' he said. 'Just a hunch.' Again he looked Skinner in the eye, and added, 'Why the questions all of a sudden, Andy? Anyone would think you're having second thoughts.'

Skinner waved his hands in a gesture of pragmatism. 'Just making sure of the lie of the land, Gus,' he said. 'My bosses are a wee bit worried about Smeaton's murder and the turf war between you and Wallace. I'd like to reassure them it won't have any knock-on effect. Which is also why I asked about Macintosh's supplier. They don't want to be stepping on anyone's toes. We've currently got all the grief we can handle.'

McMahon's face took on an expression of reassurance. 'Nothing to worry about there, Andy,' he said. 'There'll be no more trouble from Wallace, Macintosh promised me that. As for his source, I could be wrong. It might be someone down south. One thing's for sure, whoever it is won't be worrying about me.'

* * *

Sammy Reid tailed McMahon into the supermarket and slowed to walking pace as the Audi carried on to the top and parked next to a green Volkswagen Polo. As he exited and got into the Polo's passenger seat, a Mini began reversing out of the penultimate bay of a row of cars parked opposite. Reid flashed his headlights at the driver, a woman, who gave an acknowledging wave and completed her manoeuvre. Reid returned her wave, drove into the space she'd vacated, and switched off the ignition.

Reid's Corsa was screened by the end car, an ancient Rover 2000, which not only gave excellent cover, but whose windows also allowed a clear view of the Polo and the men inside. Reid took an iPhone from his pocket, activated the shutter, then picked up a copy of the *Daily Record*, and settled down to wait.

Chapter Twelve

'I don't know about you, boss,' McCann was saying, 'but I'm getting a particularly strong sense of déjà vu.' She and Knox were driving through Corstorphine on their way to St John's Road. DCS Steele had advised that Macintosh was visiting his branch in the suburb, and the detectives were travelling there to interview him.

'You're right, Arlene,' Knox replied. 'Going over pretty much the same ground does seem pointless.' He shrugged. 'Still, if that's what Steele wants…'

'Do you think Macintosh will find it credible – Wallace calling the same number McMahon was supposed to have rung on Friday?'

'Maybe. If he's as rattled as Steele believes him to be. His men *did* find the mobile he used to call Wallace, which Moran dumped. But I agree, it's a bit of a long shot.'

McCann grinned. 'Then you'll forgive me not putting a tenner on it, boss.'

Knox steered the Passat into a small car park behind a row of shops and smiled. 'Not very good odds, eh, Arlene?' he said.

The detectives exited the car and walked back to the street. Knox nodded to Macintosh's premises, a double-windowed unit at the end of the block. Baskets of petunias, geraniums and fuchsias hung from green and white awnings over both windows, underneath which a wide array of fruit and vegetables were displayed on shelving units.

Knox and McCann entered the shop, where a dozen or so customers were being served. The pair stood for a minute, and were approached by a man wearing an emerald-green apron. He addressed Knox: 'Good morning, sir. Can I be of assistance?'

'We'd like to see Mr Macintosh, please.'

'Which firm do you represent?' A pause. 'Is he expecting you?'

Knox took his warrant card from his pocket and held it discreetly at his hip. 'We're not in sales,' he said.

The man glanced at the wallet and his expression changed. 'Oh, I see,' he said, and nodded to a room at the back. 'If you'll wait here I'll go and tell him.'

He entered the back room, reappeared moments later, and waved to the door. 'Please,' he said. 'You can go through.'

Knox and McCann did so and saw Macintosh standing beside a desk near the back door. Crates and cartons occupied almost every square foot of floor space, and the detectives had to pick their way carefully around piles of stacked boxes.

'Didn't expect to see you again, Mr Knox,' Macintosh said warily. 'Not so soon, anyway.'

'You weren't at home,' Knox said. 'So we had to call on you here.'

'Well, if you couldn't await my return, it must be important.'

'It is, sir, yes.'

'Really?'

'Yes. You made a call to Hugh Wallace at his home in Broomhall Grove.' Knox said this not as a question, but as a statement of fact.

Macintosh looked aghast. 'Who told you this?' he said.

'A local saw a man throw a mobile phone from the bridge at Colinton Village. After it was retrieved the last number called was found to be Wallace's. A subsequent triangulation by the network operator places the call's source at Gillespie Road. We think it possible you made the call, and had your chauffeur dump the phone.'

Macintosh studied Knox for a long moment. 'I answered the questions you put to me yesterday as honestly as I could, Mr Knox. You originally thought I was involved with McMahon; now you suggest I'm in contact with Wallace?'

'I'm following a line of inquiry, Mr Macintosh,' Knox said. 'And giving you the right of reply.'

'If I'd taken a call from McMahon, a known drug dealer,' Macintosh said, 'and was implicated in this business as you suggest, you think I would be so stupid as to call his cohort so soon after I'd spoken to you?'

'Like I said, sir, a member of the public saw Moran throw the phone into the Water of Leith.'

'This member of the public,' Macintosh said, 'he knows Roddy?'

'I didn't speak to the witness personally,' Knox replied. 'But I gather Mr Moran's quite well known in the village. Then there's the network operator's record of the area where the call originated.'

'I'm sorry, Mr Knox, it won't wash. Anyone could have dumped that phone. And anyone could have made that call. A pedestrian, say, or someone driving on Gillespie Road. I'm afraid if you insist on pursuing this, you'll force me to bring in my lawyer.'

'No charges are being preferred at this point, Mr Macintosh. We're simply investigating the matter.'

Macintosh snorted. 'Then I was right. What you have isn't proof. If you want to speak to me again, I'll insist on my lawyer being present.'

Knox inclined his head. 'Which is entirely your prerogative, sir. However, my visit was prompted in part because of a coincidence between McMahon and Wallace.'

'What coincidence?' Macintosh asked.

'The number Wallace rang after he received a call from the phone we found,' Knox replied. 'It belonged to same west of Scotland drug dealer McMahon spoke to on Friday.'

* * *

'Think Macintosh believes you?' McCann was asking. 'About Wallace phoning Cambuslang?' The detectives were back in the car a few minutes later, heading towards the city centre.

Knox had slowed for a pedestrian crossing outside Edinburgh Zoo. The lights sequenced to green and he changed into third and accelerated gently. 'I'm fairly confident,' he replied. 'One thing for sure: he phoned McMahon from a public call box in Colinton Village, then later used the phone Moran dumped. I'd guess at some point he and McMahon discussed telecommunications security, which he's obviously concerned about.'

'Paterson hinted McMahon knew he was being flannelled,' McCann said. 'You think Macintosh's different?'

'Uh-huh, I think we succeeded in putting the wind up him. Don't forget Moran met a couple of guys at The Merlin,' Knox said. 'Both ex-cons. Steele thinks they were recruited to keep an eye on Wallace and McMahon.' He paused then added, 'No, I'm sure Macintosh is almost on the hook. The purpose of our visit was to dangle some extra bait.'

McCann grinned at the piscine analogy. 'Let's hope he bites.'

They fell silent, and a moment later Knox's iPhone rang. He placed it on the dash bracket and switched to speakers. 'Hello, Knox?'

'Hi, Jack. Ed Murray. Calling from Howdenhall forensics.'

'Hi, Ed,' Knox said. 'McCauley's trainers – you found something?'

'Yeah, but only a partial analysis. Liz and the lab ladies are carrying out further tests.'

'And?'

'Positive for Carboniferous basalt. On both heels and soles.'

'Mm-hmm,' Knox said. 'This basalt dust, Ed, it's only found in that part of the park?'

'Approximate to the area around Salisbury Crags, Jack, yes.'

'McCauley told Bill he regularly jogs between Holyrood Park Road and Duddingston Low Road. He couldn't have picked it up there?'

'The only basalt in that area is Samson's Ribs, but it's columnar, not Carboniferous.'

'Which is?'

'A harder rock formed from cooling lava, less likely to granulate.'

'Right, Ed, thanks for clarifying.'

'No problem, Jack.'

Knox ended the call and dialled Gayfield Square, where he was put through to Fulton. 'Boss?' he said.

'Just had a call from DI Murray, Bill,' Knox said. 'Forensics on McCauley's trainers tested positive.'

'So he lied? He *was* at the Crags.'

'Looks that way,' Knox replied. 'Ring St Leonards, will you? Have uniform bring him in. Arlene and I will be back in fifteen minutes. You and I will interview him again.'

'Any charge?'

'Suspected obstruction. Anything else can wait until we hear what he has to say.'

'Boss.'

* * *

'I told you, I was at the café when it opened at eight,' McCauley was saying. He and Giles Abercrombie, his solicitor, sat facing Knox and Fulton across a desk in interview room 2.

'Did anyone at Glassel House see you before you left for the café?' Knox asked.

McCauley ran his hands through his hair. 'No, I don't think so. But, like I say, the catering staff will vouch for me being there the moment they opened.'

'Eight o'clock,' Knox said. 'Still time for you to have visited Salisbury Crags before you arrived.'

'This call you received about my client following Ms Tomkins into the park,' Abercrombie said. 'It was anonymous?'

'Yes,' Knox agreed.

'A woman?'

'Yes.'

'Who wasn't prepared to give her name or come forward to be interviewed?'

'Yes.'

'You do realise, Detective Inspector Knox, a claim made in such a manner has no substance in law?'

'I do, Mr Abercrombie,' Knox said. 'However, there is the small matter of forensics.'

'Ah, yes,' Abercrombie said. 'This Carboniferous basalt – you're sure it's only found around Salisbury Crags?'

'Yes, I queried our forensics officer on that point. He was quite specific.'

Abercrombie adjusted his glasses and gave a brief nod. 'I see.'

Knox turned back to the young man facing him. 'When was the last time you went for a run in the park, Mr McCauley?'

'Monday afternoon.'

'Which part?'

'The route I always take – via Duddingston Low Road to Duddingston village and back.'

'Then how do you explain the presence of basalt dust on your trainers?'

'I can't explain it,' McCauley replied. 'But I assure you I was nowhere near Holyrood Park yesterday morning.'

Knox studied McCauley for a long moment. 'When officers brought you in the last time and asked for your trainers, you directed them to the corridor outside your dorm, where they were found beneath a radiator,' he said. 'Why?'

'I was caught in a shower on my way back from Duddingston. I put them there to dry.'

Knox checked his watch. 'Okay,' he said, then reaching over to the NEAL recorder, added, 'Interview terminated at 4.45pm.'

As he switched the machine off, Abercrombie asked, 'How do you intend to proceed, Inspector Knox?'

'Your client's free to go,' Knox replied. 'With the proviso that we may have to bring him in again. We're awaiting the results of further tests on his trainers.'

Knox nodded to a uniformed officer standing near the door, who escorted Abercrombie and McCauley from the room.

A moment or two after they'd gone, Fulton said, 'You believe he's telling the truth, boss?'

'I do, coupled with a gut feeling something's amiss,' Knox replied. 'The trainers; McCauley left them in an open corridor outside his room.'

'You think someone's attempting to frame him?'

'Possible,' Knox replied. 'The anonymous call bothers me. The woman declining to be interviewed. And the assault McCauley made on Tomkins. I've an idea if we asked her friends if they saw bruises, the answer might prove negative.'

'You want me to speak to them again?'

'Aye, better make another trip and check it out before you knock off, Bill. Take Mark with you.'

*****

Roddy Moran saw Sammy Reid and Bert Allison at The Merlin at midday on Wednesday, where they spoke for almost an hour. When he returned to relay the outcome of the meeting to his boss, Macintosh was seated in his study, ruminating on his conversation with Knox.

Moran knocked lightly and Macintosh called for him to enter.

'You saw them?' he asked when his chauffeur came into the room.

'Aye, Mr Mac,' Moran replied.

'And?'

'It's exactly as you suspected. Sammy followed McMahon to Asda at Brunstane, where he met a guy and talked for around twenty minutes. Bert had a similar experience. He tailed Wallace to the Gyle Shopping Centre, where he had a long confab with another guy.'

'I need details, Roddy,' his boss said impatiently. 'What did they look like?'

'The guys Wallace and McMahon met?'

Macintosh gave an exasperated sigh. 'Of course, who do you think I mean?'

'Sorry,' Roddy said. 'Both in their mid- to late thirties. Sammy told me the guy McMahon met looked like a farmer. Big. Casually dressed, fair hair.'

'What do you mean, "like a farmer"?'

'As if he'd been out in all weathers, like.'

'Right, ruddy-faced. Carry on.'

'The guy who met Wallace was more like a biker; leather jacket, long hair, bearded.'

'Okay, let's get down to details about McMahon's guy. Who arrived first?'

'He was already there when Sammy followed McMahon into the supermarket. Parked at a verge at the top end in a green VW Polo. Sammy says McMahon took the space alongside, got out and slipped into the Polo's passenger seat. Like I said, they talked for about twenty minutes.'

'And Wallace?'

'Bert told me it was pretty much the same at the Gyle. The bearded guy was waiting in a maroon Fiesta. Wallace arrived in his Jag, parked beside it, and got into the passenger seat.'

'How long did they talk?'

'Similar length of time. Twenty minutes, half an hour.'

'Your guys got the numbers of the two cars?'

Moran nodded and took a slip of paper from his pocket and handed it over. 'As you can see, Mr Mac, both include the letters "SG". I checked online; it's exclusive to the Glasgow area.'

Chapter Thirteen

Macintosh had Moran drive him to Colinton Village, where his chauffeur parked while he revisited the phone box. Macintosh took a number of pound coins from his pocket, placed them on the shelf beside the telephone, and dialled a number.

A few moments later a voice with a Geordie accent answered, 'Aye?'

Macintosh pushed another coin into the slot. 'Lionel?' A short pause. 'It's Tosh.'

'Aye, Tosh, man. How's it going?'

'Wee bit of a problem, Lionel.'

'Your delivery? Henry told me he had a problem with traffic yesterday. Accident on the bypass.'

'No, he wasn't all that late. I'm calling about something else.'

'Aye?'

'Aye, McMahon and Wallace. They're talking to an outfit in the west of Scotland. I think they're getting ready to jump ship.'

'You're sure?'

'Yeah, Lionel, pretty positive.' Macintosh went on to relate the events of the past two days, including Knox's hints about his distributors' phone calls. 'I got a couple of Roddy's mates to follow them,' he continued, 'usual procedure: they rendezvoused in supermarket car parks. McMahon at Brunstane, Wallace at the Gyle.'

'The meetings were pre-arranged?'

'Looks that way.'

There was a long silence at the other end of the line, then: 'That Wallace bastard and his dispute with McMahon. And if that wasn't bad enough, now they're planning to desert us.' A pause. 'You're sure the police don't suspect your involvement? This Knox guy seeing you twice; you think he's just covering the bases?'

'Almost sure of it, Lionel. They've nothing that'll stick. You know my history. Smeaton's shooting was like poking a wasp's nest with a stick; anyone with drugs in their background will be on their radar.'

'And the calls Knox said your guy's made, you think that's kosher?'

'Well, the meetings at Brunstane and the Gyle back it up,' Macintosh replied. 'I've had dealings with him before. He's always played it straight.'

'Okay, Tosh. I'll sort something out and get back to you. Leave it with me.'

* * *

'The police picked up Fraser,' Rebecca Ryan was saying. She was sitting at the edge of her bed, sipping coffee. 'I hear they took his trainers, too,' she went on. 'I think they suspect him.'

Her friend Louise was looking idly through the dorm window. She shrugged, then turned and said, 'You told the detectives a lie, Becky.'

'What lie?' Ryan asked.

'That you were sleeping when Clare left to go jogging. You know that's not true.'

Ryan placed the cup on her lap and gave Louise a blank look. 'Why bring that up?' she said. 'You know I only said it to protect you.'

'Always looking out for me, aren't you?' Louise gave a little sneer. 'I don't know why.'

Ryan flushed with anger. 'You're being deliberately provocative. We followed Clare into the park. I couldn't tell them that.'

'Why not?'

'Because at one point you and I...' Her voice trailed off.

'Separated?' Louise said. 'Why can't you bring yourself to say it, Becky? You told them you saw David and Clare in the café together. Why didn't you tell them I had a sleepless night, couldn't wait any longer, and had to confront her?' A pause. 'And that you were in the park, too?'

'But if I had told them that, they'd have suspected...'

'That I killed her? You think that, don't you?'

'Of course not. You carried on then, but...'

'So you can't be sure, can you?' Louise said. 'The fog. You couldn't see anything. You were frightened in case you slipped over the edge yourself.'

'I know, but you didn't... you couldn't...'

'Quite a conundrum, isn't it, Becky? Not knowing if your best friend's a killer?'

* * *

When Knox arrived at the office he was intercepted by Hathaway. 'DS Warburton said to let you know DCS Steele's in his office, boss,' he told Knox. 'He'd like you to see him as soon as you can.'

'Where is Warburton?' Knox asked.

'Gone to the canteen I think,' Fulton said.

McCann looked across from her desk and added, 'Cleared out to give you a wee bit of room, boss. The undercover guys are in there with the DCS.'

'To give a sitrep, most likely.' Knox then turned to Fulton and said, 'How'd you get on at the Pollock Halls, Bill?'

'Spoke to Ms Adler and Ms Baird,' Fulton said. 'The other girl, Rebecca Ryan, was out.'

'And?'

'Confirmed your suspicions, boss. The girls assured me they saw no bruising.'

'Okay,' Knox said. 'Which makes a detailed analysis of McCauley's trainers all the more important. Give DI Murray a ring, will you? Ask if there's any chance of getting the results back today.'

'Boss.'

Knox turned and crossed to Warburton's office, knocked, and heard Steele's voice: 'Come in.'

He entered and saw the DCS behind Warburton's desk. As before, DS Skinner and DS Hammond were seated near the window.

Steele waved to the vacant chair opposite. 'Please, DI Knox, take a seat.'

As Knox complied, Steele added, 'Thought you'd be interested in an update.' He smiled. 'Your interviews with Macintosh appear to have done the trick.'

'Sir?' Knox said.

Steele nodded to the undercover officers. 'DS Skinner and DS Hammond met McMahon and Wallace yesterday. At two separate locations. I'm pleased to report both meetings were witnessed by Moran's cohorts.' Steele waved a hand towards Skinner. 'Keith?'

Skinner leaned forward in his chair and addressed Knox: 'I'd arranged to see McMahon at Asda Supermarket at 11am yesterday. His Audi A6 arrived at 10.57, followed by a Vauxhall Corsa, which parked in a row of cars opposite, other side of an old Rover 2000. I identified him from the description given by the team who saw him at The Merlin. It was Sammy Reid.'

Steele flicked a finger towards DS Hammond. 'Steve?'

'Same at the Gyle, sir,' Hammond told Knox. 'As Wallace drove in I saw a Mondeo a few hundred yards behind… Bert Allison. He parked a short distance away and remained there while I talked to Wallace. Pretended to read a copy of *The Sun*, but every now and then I caught him sneaking a furtive glance in our direction.'

'Keith and Steve set up the meeting to finalise our "deal" with Wallace and McMahon,' Steele said, 'in their guise as members of a west of Scotland drug cartel. Offered to supply at ten grand a kilo less than they're currently paying Macintosh. Both agreed the transaction.'

'So,' Knox asked, 'how do you plan to proceed?'

'The main object of interest is Macintosh's supplier. We've pretty much everything we need on Wallace and McMahon. DS Skinner and DS Hammond's cars are rigged with recording devices, and in the course of several conversations they've given us enough ammunition.

'It's Macintosh's supplier who's proving a hard nut to crack,' Steele continued. He reached into a briefcase and took out a small digital recorder, which he placed on the desk, then pressed the play button and added, 'This is a recording of a telephone call made by Macintosh at a public phone box at Colinton Village. As you'll hear, the recipient is a native of the north-east of England.'

After the recording ended, Steele said, 'We attempted a trace, without success. Our tech people tell us it was received somewhere in the north-east, but filtered through an obscure internet link. Quite sophisticated, apparently – continuously reroutes calls back and forth between dozens of mobile providers. And, of course, impossible to trace.'

'But what about this Lionel guy, sir?' Knox said. 'Wouldn't Northumbria Police be able to assist?'

'They already are,' Steele replied. '"Lionel", they tell us, is most likely an alias. He might be linked to one of the bigger outfits in the area, but they're not sure. We've sent them a copy of the tape, anyway, which they'll check with voice-matching software. However, there's an opportunity to make an arrest in the meantime.' He tapped the recorder and went on, 'Just before he rings off, he tells Macintosh he's going to, quote, "sort something out".'

'You think he'll come up here?' Knox asked.

'Accompanied by enforcers, almost certainly,' Steele replied.

'So you'll be keeping tabs on Wallace and McMahon?'

'Yes,' Steele replied. 'We'll have a covert team, ready in place to tail Lionel and whoever turns up back in the north-east. With the help of Northumbria Police, we'll sever this particular snake's head for good and for all.'

'And Macintosh?' Knox asked.

'Ah, yes, Macintosh,' Steele said. 'Well, we've some pretty incriminating stuff on tape, of course, but we require more to ensure a watertight conviction. We've never actually nailed down his complete chain of supply. Where the drugs are delivered – where they're stored before being passed on, that sort of thing.' He shook his head. 'The most obvious place is his shops – you interviewed him at his St John's Road branch... saw the stock room?'

'Yes, sir,' Knox agreed. 'Pretty cluttered.'

'But Macintosh isn't that stupid,' Steele said. 'Curiously, a great deal of his produce is purchased from a warehouse in South Shields and trucked up the A1. We originally surmised that the delivery lorry might be intercepted en route, where – with or without the driver's knowledge – boxes in Macintosh's order are opened and drugs hidden.

'With this in mind, we made a note of the wholesaler and had the Ministry of Transport set up an HGV stop at the Old Craighall interchange, the route the company's drivers take when approaching the city. The MOT officials pulled in a few lorries, then our target arrived: a five-ton wagon belonging to Cummings Fruit & Veg of South Shields.

'They gave the vehicle a thorough going-over, then had the driver open the back. Two of our team got inside and inspected the load, giving particular attention to Macintosh's order. They checked crate after crate, box after box, but found nothing.'

'Maybe you were just unlucky with the lorry you stopped, sir,' Knox said. 'Your theory may be correct, but it's possible Macintosh's drugs are shipped only once or twice a week.'

Steele nodded. 'Yes, I've considered that,' he said. 'And of course the alternative would be to get a warrant – go in mob-handed, raid all three shops. Which we may yet do.' Steele cleared his throat. 'Trouble is, we might get Macintosh, but miss out on the one we're really after. You see, Knox, we think Lionel's outfit is supplying most of the Lothians.'

Knox nodded. 'I see, sir. Bit of a quandary.'

'It is,' Steele said, then straightened in his chair and stood. 'Still, your interactions have proved useful. The fact our Geordie friend is sufficiently exercised to come to Edinburgh might be our best break yet.' He nodded to the door and added, 'Okay, Knox, that's all for now. Any developments, I'll let you know.'

Chapter Fourteen

As Knox came back into the office, Hathaway handed him a sheet of paper. 'DS Beattie dropped this off while you were in with the DCS, boss,' he said. 'I think it's updated forensics on McCauley's trainers.'

As Knox studied the report, the two remaining members of his team looked across from their desks.

'Anything interesting, boss?' McCann said.

'Aye,' Fulton added. 'Liz tipped us the wink that she'd found something.'

'Ascorbic acid,' Knox said.

Fulton gave him a puzzled look. 'Eh?'

'Vitamin C – ascorbic acid. The report says the soil sample was subjected to a second test and minute quantities were found.'

Fulton shook his head. 'How is that possible,' he said, 'unless…'

'Unless whoever murdered Clare is trying to implicate McCauley,' McCann said.

'You mean–'

McCann interrupted, 'I mean the killer filled an empty vitamin C container with Carboniferous soil. Took it back to the Pollock Halls and spread it into the soles of McCauley's trainers.'

'It fits,' Knox said. 'He told us it rained on his way back from Duddingston. Left them to dry beside a radiator in the corridor, which is where they were found when we picked him up.'

'Which begs the question,' Hathaway said, 'who did the bottle belong to?'

'I think we've already spoken to her,' Knox said.

'You mean the woman who rang?' Fulton said.

Knox nodded. 'Whoever it was knew we'd bring McCauley in, find his trainers.'

McCann dipped her head in a gesture of agreement. 'The killer came back from the park, waited until he'd left for the café, and planted the soil.'

'She'd have been taking a risk of being seen on the men's floor,' Hathaway said.

'Maybe,' Knox agreed. 'Unless she waited until later, after the men left to attend lectures.'

'But that would have meant missing her own classes,' Hathaway countered.

'Not necessarily.'

'Oh, I forgot, boss. Neither Fiona Baird nor Sofia Adler left Glassel House on Tuesday.'

No one said anything for a long moment, then Fulton broke the silence. 'You think it might have been a woman?'

Knox waved the forensics report. 'Well, I think we all agree McCauley's trainers were tampered with. Which leaves us with the chap Clare was seeing most recently – David Martin.' He paused for a moment, then addressed Hathaway, 'The prints of the photos from Clare Tomkins' phone, Mark. The only people in them are those you interviewed? No one else in their circle – this Parker, for example?'

'Dave Martin's room-mate?' Hathaway said. 'No, the only folk in the photos are Martin and McCauley, her own room-mates, and the two girls next door.'

'The *two* girls next door?' Knox said. 'I thought you only spoke to one?'

'Rebecca Ryan shares her dorm with a girl called Sandrine Cudlipp, boss. She had to return to Leicester to attend a funeral.'

'When did she leave?'

'Monday morning, I think.'

'H-mm,' Knox said, then nodded towards Fulton. 'Okay, Bill. You and Mark had better return to the student complex. Reinterview Clare's room-mates and Rebecca Ryan. Speak to the Cudlipp girl, too, if she's back. More importantly, though, reinterview David Martin and the other lad, Parker. See if they can shine any light on comings and goings on their floor. You never know, somebody might have witnessed something.'

'Boss,' Fulton said.

As Knox placed the forensic report on his in tray, his phone rang. He checked the screen and saw the call was from Turley.

'Hi, Alex,' he said.

'Afternoon, Jack,' Turley said. 'Norman Smeaton – you asked me to find out when they'll let his wife have his body?'

'Oh, yes, Alex,' Knox said. 'How'd you get on?'

'I spoke to Lorna.' Knox said nothing, and Turley added, '*Professor* Lorna Wright, the pathologist in charge?'

'Yes, Alex, sorry. I recall.'

'She tells me they'll conclude the PM today. The body will be released tomorrow.'

'That's fine, Alex, I appreciate that.'

'Another thing, Jack. Before you go.'

'Yes, Alex?'

'The Tomkins woman. I found a deep scratch behind her left ear. I think it may have been gauged with a fingernail. The nature of the scratch would suggest the fingernail was particularly long.'

'A woman's?' Knox asked.

'Men generally prefer their nails shorter,' Turley said, 'I'd say it's more likely than not.'

'Interesting. That might prove helpful.'

'What I'm here for, Jack.'

Knox ended the call and keyed in a number. It rang for a moment or two, then a female voice answered. 'Hello?'

'Lisa?' Knox said.

'No. Her sister Laura.'

'Oh, I see,' Knox said. 'Lisa's not at home?'

'No, she's at the shops. You're police? They're releasing Norrie? She told me you might call.'

'Yes. I'm Detective Inspector Knox. Would you tell her the pathology lab at Gartcosh have concluded the postmortem? Lisa can arrange for Norman's body to be picked up tomorrow.'

'Oh, she'll be relieved,' Laura said. 'She was sitting about the house fretting. Why I told her to go out and do some shopping.'

'I see,' Knox said. 'You'll tell her when she gets back?'

'I promise,' Laura replied. 'Thanks for letting us know.'

Knox ended the call, returned the iPhone to his pocket, and saw DCI Warburton approach. 'Got a minute, Jack?' he said.

'Yes, sir.'

'We can speak in my office. DCS Steele and the others have left.'

Knox followed his boss into the room and Warburton sat at his desk and indicated a chair opposite.

'I was in the canteen when the duty sergeant told me I had a call,' Warburton said. 'It was from Henry Slater, governor at Saughton Prison.'

Knox held Warburton's gaze, but said nothing.

'It's Derek Tate, Jack. He was found hanged.'

'Where?' Knox asked. 'When?'

'In his cell. After lights out last night.'

Knox shook his head. 'Suicide?'

'As soon as the governor contacted us, he was put through to our North West office. A couple of officers were sent out from West End Police Station at Torphichen Place, DCI Madden and DS Gray. Only preliminary inquiries so far, but it looks that way. Tate was alone in his cell; the door was locked.'

Knox made a face. 'Awkward.'

'Sorry, Jack, I'm not with you.'

'This drugs inquiry; Macintosh.'

'Macintosh?'

'During my first interview,' Knox said, 'Macintosh talked about Tate and commiserated about Yvonne's murder. He knew Tate was in Saughton, said he had better watch his back, that rapists and killers of women are treated with contempt and should expect retribution.'

'But surely Macintosh couldn't be implicated in any way?'

'I don't know, sir. Moran, his chauffeur-cum-bodyguard served time in Saughton, as did two others who've been working for Macintosh lately; Sam Reid and Albert Allison.'

Warburton shook his head. 'I don't think he's behind anything untoward, Jack. As I say, Tate had been in his cell, the door was locked.'

'I know, sir,' Knox said, 'I'd like to check it out, just the same.'

'You want to go to the West End office, speak to Madden and Gray?'

'To set my mind at rest, sir, yes. If I you don't mind.'

Warburton reached over and picked up his telephone handset. 'Okay,' he said. 'I'll give their office a ring, arrange an appointment.'

* * *

'It was just as Governor Slater told your boss,' Madden was saying. 'Tate was found in his cell after lights out.' Two hours had passed since Warburton called and the DI and his colleague, DS Kirsty Gray, were seated opposite Knox and McCann in a side office at West End Police Station.

Madden was dark-haired and thickset and in his mid-forties. Gray, tall and slim and at least ten years younger. She nodded agreement and said, 'A prison officer had been on the landing. He witnessed Tate enter his cell a few minutes before lockdown.'

'And Tate was the only occupant?' Knox asked.

'Yes,' Madden said. 'Had been since his admission, apparently.'

'When was he discovered?' Knox asked.

'Regular check by the watch officer at 11pm,' Madden replied. 'Looked through the viewing hatch and saw Tate dangling from the end of a length of rope attached to a hook on the window.'

'How did he come by the rope?' McCann asked.

'We're not a hundred per cent sure,' Gray replied. 'But we do know it must've been acquired this week. The staff do a cell check every Friday.'

'A senior officer thinks he picked it up in the metal shop, where he worked,' Madden said. 'Their steel tubes come bundled; same variety of hemp.'

'Hmm,' Knox said. 'Do you know if he'd been under strain? Anyone threatening him?'

'First thing we checked,' Madden replied. 'His mental health; if he'd been depressed, undergone mood swings, anything like that.'

'And?' Knox said.

'Well, as far as the staff are aware, no,' Madden replied.

'But we asked around,' Gray said. 'Spoke to prisoners he worked with in the metal shop. Most were unhelpful, but an older chap called Malachy told us in confidence that Tate had been in a punch-up in the last few days.'

'What happened?'

'It took place in the yard,' Gray said. 'He was set upon by a couple of the younger lads. Prison officers stepped in before it got out of hand. When asked what the row was about, all those involved – Tate included – clammed up. The warders involved believed it'd been a dispute over cigarettes.'

'But you suspect something else?'

'Yes,' Madden said. 'Malachy told us the pair had a particular reason for their animosity. One had an aunt who'd been raped, the other a sister who was stabbed by her spouse.'

'So Tate *was* under duress?' Knox said. 'He was being targeted?'

Madden nodded. 'I think so. And for that reason our inquiry hasn't concluded. We didn't press Malachy when we spoke to him – too many other inmates to witness the exchange. So we arranged with the governor to speak to him again tomorrow, in private. We'll attempt to discover who attacked Tate in the yard.'

'I'd be interested if there were any previous incidents or threats of violence towards Tate,' Knox said. 'Or if the fracas in the yard was the first time he'd been targeted. And also if a guy called Moran's name was mentioned in connection with a phone call.'

'Made to the prison?'

'Yes.'

'Right,' Madden said, 'we'll check that.'

'Okay,' Knox said, getting to his feet. 'I'd appreciate if you could update me on the outcome.'

'Of course,' Madden replied. 'I'll give you a ring after we speak to Malachy.'

'Thanks,' Knox replied. 'And I appreciate your seeing us at short notice.'

'No problem,' Madden said.

* * *

'The stooshie in the yard, boss,' McCann was saying, 'you think it took place after our first interview with Macintosh?'

The detectives had only recently left West End Police Station and were driving through the Grassmarket in central Edinburgh.

'Too much of a coincidence for my liking,' Knox replied. 'Then there's Moran, Reid and Allison... all former Saughton inmates.'

'Yet it's strange,' McCann added, 'you wouldn't have thought Macintosh would concern himself with...'

'The murder of a policewoman – in particular the fiancée of an officer conducting an investigation against him?'

'Sorry, boss, I didn't mean–'

'It's okay, Arlene, similar thoughts crossed my mind.' Knox shrugged. 'The only explanation I can come up with is that it's like the letter he wrote to the Chief Constable back in '97. An attempt to ingratiate himself.'

'Things might go easier for him if he plays Mr Nice Guy?'

'Something like that. Psychology was never my strong suit.' Knox shook his head. 'Guess we'll have to wait till Madden gets back to us.'

He glanced at his watch, placed his iPhone on the dash, and keyed a number. 'I'm going to give Bill a ring,' he said. 'See how he and Mark are doing with the Pollock Hall interviews.'

The speakers crackled with the dial tone for a moment, then they heard the sound of Fulton's voice: 'Boss?'

'Hi, Bill.' Knox signalled right and turned the Passat into Candlemaker Row. 'Where are you?'

'Still at Glassel House,' Fulton replied. 'Mark and I have just left Clare Tomkins' room-mates, Ms Adler and Ms Baird. We're just about to reinterview Rebecca Ryan; the girl next door.'

'Any joy so far?'

'Only one thing – the vitamin C,' Fulton said. 'Ms Adler reckons the girl with Ryan, Sandrine Cudlipp, uses vitamin supplements.'

'Is she back yet?'

'The girls in 2c aren't sure,' Fulton replied. 'We'll discover that in a minute.'

'And Tomkins' room-mates,' Knox said. 'Any clue who might've tampered with McCauley's trainers?'

'No, boss. They saw nothing untoward.'

'Right, Bill,' Knox said. 'You and Mark see Ryan; and Cudlipp, if she's back. Arlene and I are only a ten-minute drive away. We'll talk to Martin and Parker. Save a bit of time.'

'Fine, boss.'

Chapter Fifteen

'Oh!' Rebecca Ryan said as she answered Fulton's Knock. 'Didn't expect to see you again. Not so soon, anyway.'

'There's been a wee bit of a development, Miss,' Fulton said. 'We're here again checking it out… mind if we come in?'

Ryan held open the door. 'Not at all,' she said, waving Fulton and Hathaway inside. 'You mentioned a development – it concerns Fraser McCauley?'

Fulton gave Ryan a searching look. 'Perhaps,' he said. 'Why do you ask?'

Ryan smiled. 'The Pollock Halls is a pretty close community. Tongues wag. Fraser was seen leaving Glassel House accompanied by police officers.' She paused then added, 'He was arrested?'

'No, Miss,' Fulton said sternly. 'He was helping us with our inquiries. And has since been released.'

'"Helping with your inquiries",' Ryan said. 'That's a euphemism, isn't it? Fraser's a suspect?'

Fulton ignored the question. 'We've just come from your neighbours' dorm – Ms Baird and Ms Adler. I was asking if they witnessed unusual activity between the ground floor – the men's dorms – and here.'

'I'm not sure what you mean by unusual activity.'

'I mean any resident of the first floor who was in the vicinity of G7 on Monday night, or anytime on Tuesday.'

'A woman?'

'Yes.'

'This has to do with Fraser's trainers?'

Fulton studied Ryan for a long moment. 'What do you know about Mr McCauley's trainers?'

'Only that your officers picked them up at the same time Fraser was taken,' Ryan said. 'Like I say, Detective, tongues wag – it's common knowledge.'

Fulton glanced at Hathaway, who gave a barely perceptible shrug. 'When we spoke to you on Tuesday you told us you use a bicycle,' Fulton said. 'Where do you keep it?'

'There's a shed on the ground floor,' Ryan said. 'Students who cycle keep their machines there – why do you ask?'

'No particular reason,' Fulton replied. 'Both levels of the building – the men's dorms on the ground floor, and the women's on this floor – are accessed via the same entrance. Anyone heading to the upper floor has a clear view of the men's landing before accessing the stairs. I don't suppose you saw anything unusual on Monday or Tuesday?'

Ryan shook her head. 'No.'

'Your friend, Ms Cudlipp,' Hathaway said. 'Any word on when she might get back?'

'I asked Ms Adams earlier,' Ryan replied. 'She told me Sandrine phoned this morning. She'll arrive in Edinburgh later this evening.'

'Ms Cudlipp,' Fulton said. 'Does she use vitamins?'

Ryan blanched. 'Vitamins?'

'Yes,' Fulton said. 'Supplements – vitamin C for example.'

Ryan's eyes went to a table in the corner of the room, on which a couple of bottles stood. 'Oh, yes,' she said.

'Yes, Sandrine's susceptible to colds. She's sure they help to prevent them.'

* * *

Wallace drove into Morrisons supermarket at Granton and saw the red Volvo 240 already parked. As he pulled into a space alongside, its driver exited his vehicle, opened the Jaguar's nearside door, and slid into the passenger seat.

The man thrust a large, bulky envelope into his hand and said, 'Thirty grand, Shug. Mostly twenties this time, like you asked for.'

Wallace gave him a disdainful look. 'The higher the denomination the better, Willie; easier to count.'

'I remembered, Shug,' the man replied. 'No fivers.'

'Good,' Wallace said, then looked over his shoulder. 'Your package is on the back seat. Under the travel rug.'

The man reached over, pulled aside a tartan blanket, and took a shoebox-sized parcel. 'Right, Shug, thanks. See you.' He exited, got back into the Volvo and started the engine, and drove off.

Wallace consulted his Rolex Daytona and gave a smug smile. The entire transaction had taken under two minutes.

His mobile rang at that moment and he glanced at the screen, which displayed: *Caller unknown*. Wallace tapped the *accept* icon. 'Hello?'

'Shug Wallace?' A male voice. One he couldn't remember having heard before.

'Aye, who's that?'

'You don't know me, Shug, I'm a friend of Steve Hammond's.'

'Oh, right. He said he'd get in touch – you're with the outfit?'

'You could say that, yeah.'

'So,' Wallace said. 'What's happening?'

'There's been a few developments. We need to talk.'

'Where?'

'Where are you now?'

'Granton.'

'Okay. Drive up to Blackhall. I'll see you in Sainsbury's car park in half an hour.'

'How will I know you?' Wallace asked.

'You drive a maroon Jag, right?'

'Right.'

'Okay. I'll look for you there.'

* * *

Wallace drove into the car park, selected a vacant bay near the entrance, then stopped and switched off the engine. The cars nearby had no occupants, save for an elderly woman in a blue Honda Jazz who was studying a till receipt. After a moment she placed the list in the glove box together with her reading glasses, started the car, and drove off.

As Wallace watched her depart, he saw a Vauxhall Astra cruise into the space she'd vacated. A stocky man in his early fifties exited, glanced in Wallace's direction, walked over and opened the Jaguar's passenger door, and got inside.

'Shug,' he said. 'Glad you've such a classy motor. I'd never have recognised you from your picture.'

Wallace bristled. The man had an air about him that set alarm bells ringing. 'What picture?' he said. 'And who the hell are *you*?'

'I told you on the phone, Shug. Steve Hammond's friend.'

'No, you're not. You're a cop.'

'Aye, that too. But then, so is Steve.'

Wallace paled. 'I don't know what you mean. Steve's, Steve's—'

'Our mutual friend, Hammond? A member of a drug outfit from Cambuslang? Offered you smack at ten grand a kilo less than Macintosh, did he?' The man gave a snort of derision, and added, 'Sorry, Shug, I'm afraid you've been the victim of a cunning wee deception.'

111

Wallace's face crumpled. 'A fucking set-up,' he said. 'I should've guessed.'

'Aye, you were set up all right. When you shot your mouth off to our hairy DS, there was a recorder in the back of his car, taping your every word. Your jaiket's hanging from a shoogly peg, son.'

Wallace said nothing.

'But… not to worry. I came to offer you a way out.'

'A way out?'

'Aye.' A pause. 'If you choose to take it.'

'I still don't know who you are,' Wallace said.

The man flicked open his warrant card and flashed it in Wallace's face. 'Detective Inspector Paterson… Police Scotland Narcotics Squad. More importantly – and lucky for you – soon to be *ex*-DI Paterson. I'm taking early retirement. And giving you, my friend, an opportunity to contribute towards my pension fund.'

* * *

Knox's press on the bell push at dorm G7 was answered by Clive Parker, who held the door open. 'You're here to talk to Dave?' he asked.

'Yes,' Knox replied. 'I'm Detective Inspector Knox and this is Detective Sergeant McCann. We're following up on our colleagues' visit earlier.'

'Sure,' Parker replied. 'Come in.'

Knox and McCann entered and saw Martin sitting on his bed, a textbook balanced on his knees. He glanced up at the detectives and put the book aside. 'Sorry I wasn't able to respond all that well to your colleague,' he said. 'I was a bit overcome.'

Knox dipped his head in acknowledgement. 'Nothing to apologise for,' he said, then motioned to a couple of chairs. 'You mind if we sit down?'

'No, sorry,' Martin said. 'Go ahead.'

As they did so Parker indicated a table in the corner, on which an electric kettle sat together with mugs, sugar bowl and carton of milk. 'I was just making tea,' he said. 'Would you like some?'

Knox shook his head. 'Not for us, thanks.'

Parker nodded, went to the table and switched on the kettle, which immediately came to the boil.

'You wanted to ask about Clare?' Martin said.

'Yes,' Knox agreed. 'DS Fulton told us you and she went to the cinema on Monday night?'

'Yes. The Dominion at Church Hill, the early performance. We stopped off at The Wine Glass in East Preston Street on the way back, had a couple of drinks.'

'And that was the last time you saw her?'

'Yes. We'd arranged to meet in the café at seven on Tuesday night.' Martin swallowed. 'I never imagined then…'

'So the two of you were dating regularly?' McCann asked.

'Over the last three weeks, yes.'

Parker came over at that moment, placed a mug of tea on Martin's bedside table, then sat on the edge of his own bed, cupping a second mug in his hands. 'We heard Fraser McCauley is a suspect,' he said. 'Is that true?'

'Why do you ask?' Knox said.

'The rumour was he'd been taken to the police station.'

'That doesn't necessarily imply guilt, Mr Parker,' Knox replied, before turning to Martin. 'Fraser dated Clare at the start of term. I take it you knew that?'

Martin nodded. 'Yes, she mentioned she'd been out with him a couple of times.'

'Did she say anything else?'

'She told me he wanted to continue seeing her.'

'But she didn't want to see him?' McCann said.

'Yes. He was miffed about it. She told me they argued.'

'But he accepted it in the end?'

'I think so.'

'She never mentioned him bothering her?'

'No, nothing like that.'

'Do you and he get on?' Knox asked.

Martin shrugged. 'McCauley? We never argued over Clare if that's what you mean. He's in the dorm next door, but I hardly ever see him.'

'We found some images of Clare on her phone,' Knox said. 'Taken with the girls in her dorm and the one adjacent. Do you know them?'

'Yes,' Martin said. 'Well, not really in a social sense – outside the campus, I mean. We'd meet in the café together with Clare sometimes, have a chat.'

'Were you seeing any of them?'

'No.'

'What about Becky?' Parker said.

'Oh, sorry,' Martin said. 'Yeah, I forgot. I went out with her once at the start of term. Before I met Clare.'

'Becky?' McCann said.

'Rebecca Ryan,' Martin replied. 'I think she and Sandrine Cudlipp share dorm 4c.'

Chapter Sixteen

'I'm worried, Louise,' Ryan was saying. 'I think you used Sandrine's empty vitamin C bottle to take a sample of soil from the cliffs.'

Fulton and Hathaway had recently departed, and Ryan sat on the edge of her bed wringing her hands. 'No doubt it was picked up when they did tests on Fraser's trainers.'

Louise looked at her friend and gave a little sneer. 'Is that so? And who was it that glanced in the direction of Sandrine's supplement bottles the moment vitamin C was mentioned?'

'I was taken by surprise,' Ryan said. 'Which doesn't alter the fact that you should have been more careful. You were bound to realise they'd look at the evidence more closely.'

Louise harrumphed. 'I don't understand why you're getting so excited. The vitamins belong to Sandrine. She'll be the one under suspicion.'

'But Sandrine returned home on Monday morning. The police will know she couldn't have had anything to do with Clare's…' Ryan paused, catching a sob rising in her throat. 'With Clare's murder.'

'Oh, for God's sake, Becky. Stop getting so damned emotional. You're forgetting I won't be here when the police return. Sandrine will be back in just a few hours. It'll be only you and her.' Louise paused. 'Just tell the truth. After all, you weren't with me when it happened, were you?'

'No.'

'Okay. Let's face facts. *Where* were you?'

'I don't know. Two or three hundred yards away, perhaps.'

'Exactly. You panicked when the fog thickened, didn't you? Frightened that you'd wander near the cliff edge and slip. What happened then?'

'You went on alone.'

'Of course. So… if the worst comes to the worst, you can tell them truthfully you had nothing to do with it, can't you?'

'But – oh, Louise, you're my best friend. I don't ever want to get you into trouble.'

Louise caressed Ryan's cheek. 'There's nothing to worry about, darling,' she said. 'Absolutely nothing at all. I won't be here.'

* * *

Wallace took a deep breath as Paterson continued, 'Now where was I, Shug? Ah, yes, you're wondering what I have? Well, I must tell you, son, it's really quite substantial. You see, in addition to DS Hammond's tapes, there's Norrie Smeaton's murder.'

'But you can't prove–'

'Ah, but I can, Shug. You see, son, murder's a *very* serious thing, no matter who the victim is. What's more, most petty first- and second-time offenders know that. When the murder squad comes calling, these fellas start quaking in their boots.

'Tommy Kennedy, for example, your spotter at Kaimes Green Crescent. I found him pretty quick. He was caught on CCTV at a chemist on Kaimes Green Row, a five-minute walk away. Wandering past checking his mobile phone, wearing a bright red baseball hat. Couple of kids playing football at the end of the crescent saw him approach from that direction immediately after the shooting. Told me where he lived.

'He folded pretty quickly when I spoke to him. Particularly when it was pointed out that being an accessory to murder carries a hefty sentence. Named you as the driver of the BMW, the man who killed Smeaton.'

'Rubbish,' Wallace protested.

'Is it, Shug? You see, not only do I have Kennedy's testimony, but also the Beamer. Tommy tells me it was stolen in central Edinburgh last week, and that it's currently in a lockup in Gracemount.

'You told him to leave it there for a few days, await your call. He was to take it to a stretch of waste ground in Burdiehouse and torch it. But it's not been torched yet, has it? Still in the lockup – your DNA all over it.' Paterson cleared his throat. 'Have I shown you enough aces yet, son?'

Wallace made a face. 'You said you were prepared to do a deal?'

'I did,' Paterson said. 'It'll cost you two hundred grand. I take it you have it?'

'I have it.'

'Good,' Paterson said. He tapped the glove box. 'I'll take a wee bit in advance. Proof of your good faith.'

'I've only got around 50k with me,' Wallace said.

'That'll do,' Paterson replied.

Wallace opened the glove box and handed over two envelopes. 'There's thirty grand in one,' he said, 'twenty in the other.'

Paterson took an empty Sainsbury's carrier bag out of his pocket and stuffed the envelopes inside. 'Ta,' he replied. 'By the way, you know Macintosh is on to you, don't you?'

'What do you mean?'

'He's aware you're chatting to Hammond – under the impression the DS is a bona fide drug dealer. Knows you're getting ready to skip.'

'Who the hell told him?'

'We did… well, not me personally. A cop called Knox, who my DCS persuaded to interview him. Knox dropped a hint; Macintosh took the bait. All part of the sting.'

'So they intend taking Macintosh out?'

'Not only Macintosh,' Paterson said. 'His entire supply chain.' He gave Wallace a pointed look. 'You know a man called Lionel?'

'Can't say I've heard of him.'

'A Geordie, somewhere in the Newcastle area?'

Wallace shook his head.

'Macintosh contacted him about you and McMahon seeking pastures new.'

Wallace snorted. 'Christ! McMahon was part of the con? You succeeded in fooling him, too?'

'"fraid so,' Paterson replied. 'Thing is, this Lionel guy isn't going to be taking it lying down. Heading north, no doubt, and mob-handed. You and McMahon are likely to be on the receiving end of a fair degree of unpleasantness.'

'Why are you telling me this?'

'To protect my investment. Not in my best interest to see you come to harm, is it?' A pause. 'You've somewhere to go?'

'I don't understand.'

'A place to lie low for a while. You married?'

'My wife left me.'

'I see. You've got a place?'

'Aye, a wee flat in Leith.'

'Good,' Paterson said. 'I'd steer clear of Broomhall Grove and any other haunts for a few days.'

Wallace was silent for a long moment.

'You're wondering where you're going to source your gear once Macintosh and Lionel are taken down?' Paterson said.

'Had crossed my mind, yeah. Particularly as I'm into you for another hundred and fifty grand.'

'I've been planning my retirement for a while, Shug, so don't think I haven't given it a considerable amount of thought.' A pause. 'There's a guy in the west who'll supply you. But, like I say, you'll need to lie low for a while; four or five weeks. I'll ring you with his number once things settle down. Oh, and by the way – I wouldn't worry about Hammond's tapes. There's nothing on them a good brief won't have thrown out of court.'

Wallace gave a thin smile. 'The other 150k I owe you; doesn't wipe my sheet clean, does it?'

Paterson returned his smile and reached for the door handle. 'The price of doing business, son,' he said. 'The price of doing business.'

* * *

When Knox and McCann left Glassel House they found Fulton and Hathaway waiting in the car park, where the detectives compared notes.

'Ryan told us her room-mate suffers from colds,' Fulton said. 'Takes vitamin C. We saw a couple of supplement bottles on Cudlipp's bedside table.'

'This girl,' Knox said, 'she left for Leicester on Monday morning?'

'Yes,' Hathaway agreed. 'A close relative's funeral.'

'She's not back yet?'

'No, boss, Ryan's up there on her own,' Fulton said, then added, 'How did you get on with Martin?'

'Nothing much to add to what he told you, except…'

Fulton looked at him expectantly. 'Aye?'

'Ryan,' Knox said. 'Her name came up again.'

'Dave Martin,' McCann explained. 'They dated at the beginning of term.'

'Odd that she never mentioned it to us,' Fulton said.

'Hmm,' Knox said. 'Any idea when Ms Cudlipp will be back, did Ryan say?'

'Ms Adams, the block supervisor, told her it should be sometime this evening.'

Knox checked his watch. 'Okay. I'd like to tie up these interviews tonight if I can.' He turned to McCann. 'Arlene, Mark can drive you back to Gayfield Square to pick up your car and you can both call it a day. Bill and I will hang around a bit, speak to Cudlipp. We'll get a cup of tea if the campus café's still open. Catch up with the two of you in the morning.'

'Okay, boss,' McCann said.

As Hathaway drove off, Knox and Fulton walked into Pollock Halls' main building, where a receptionist directed them to the staff dining room. Knox and Fulton ordered tea and BLT sandwiches, and had almost finished when Adams entered the room.

She recognised Fulton and walked to their table. 'Shona at reception said I'd find you here,' she said.

'Yes,' Fulton replied, 'We were having a cup of tea while we were waiting.' He waved towards Knox. 'This is Detective Inspector Knox. Ms Adams is Glassel House's superintendent, boss.'

Knox gave the woman an acknowledging nod. 'Ms Adams.'

'They tell me it's a murder inquiry?' she said gravely.

'I'm afraid so,' Knox said. 'Has Ms Cudlipp returned?'

'Yes,' Adams said. 'That's why I'm here. Shona phoned, said you were waiting to speak to her.' She paused then added, 'She's just back.'

Chapter Seventeen

McMahon's last stop for the day was at Morrisons car park on Gilmerton Road. Teatime on Thursdays the supermarket was quite busy, but he found a parking space relatively easily. Jenkins, the pusher he'd come to meet, was already parked.

McMahon flashed his lights as he drew up behind the Mondeo. Jenkins raised a thumb in response, exited the Ford, walked back to McMahon's Audi, opened the passenger door, and slid into the passenger seat.

'Aye, Gus,' Jenkins said. 'Busy.'

'Morrisons, or you?' McMahon said.

Jenkins gave a little laugh. 'This place is always busy on Thursdays. A lot of folk get paid.' A short pause. 'No, I meant me.'

He took an envelope from inside his bomber jacket and McMahon nodded to the glove box. 'In there.'

As Jenkins opened it and placed the envelope inside, McMahon said, 'How much?'

'Better than last week, Gus. A couple of hundred shy of 44k.'

McMahon nodded. 'Good, Manny. Almost five grand up.' He nodded towards the rear of the car. 'The boot's open. Your gear's in a Morrisons bag. Better not hang about.'

'Righto, Gus. See you next week. Same place?'

'Unless my text message says different.'

Jenkins exited, went to the Audi's boot and extracted a carrier bag, waved on the way back to his Mondeo, and drove off.

McMahon started the car, selected first gear, and had begun to move forward when a Land Rover Discovery quickly reversed into the space Jenkins had vacated.

McMahon cursed and pressed on the horn, but the Land Rover continued to reverse. A tow bar at the rear of the vehicle was now dangerously close to the Audi's front bumper, forcing McMahon to back up.

'Arsehole!' McMahon shouted, then glanced over his shoulder with the intention of reversing, except he was prevented from doing so by a Mitsubishi Shogun, which straddled the space between cars on either side, blocking his exit.

'What the f—' McMahon said. He was about to get out when the nearside door opened and a man got into the passenger seat. Almost immediately the rear doors also opened and two hefty-looking individuals got in the back.

'You're a hard man to find, Gus,' the man in the passenger seat said. He was balding, and not quite as big as his companions. He spoke quietly and firmly, like someone accustomed to giving orders. If McMahon had to guess his age, he would say early to mid-forties.

By now he'd regained his composure. 'What's the game?' the man said.

'I could ask you the same question, Gus.'

'What question?'

'What game you're playing.'

McMahon shook his head. 'I'm not with you.'

'You really don't remember me, do you?'

McMahon studied the man for a moment. Broad face; square jawline. Thin pencil moustache covering his upper lip. He'd heard the voice before, too – a slight Geordie accent. Not pronounced, but definitely detectable.

Suddenly it came back to him – Lionel Levy, henchman to Danny Lawson, the Sunderland dealer who'd supplied Wallace and him ten years before.

'Lionel?' McMahon said.

'Light bulb moment, eh?' the man said.

'I didn't recognise you.'

Levy ran a hand over his head. 'Aye, man. Lost a wee bit of hair since I saw you last. Wee bit of weight as well.'

'You were with Lawson?'

'Aye. Danny's dead – heart attack. I head the outfit now. Which brings me to why we're here. Macintosh tells me you and Wallace are getting ready to do a runner.'

McMahon gasped in surprise. 'Macintosh – you know him?' he said.

Levy gave a sarcastic laugh. 'Aye, you can say that again.'

At that moment, the penny dropped. 'You're his supplier?' McMahon said.

'Aye, bonny lad,' Levy said. Then, suddenly serious, he added, 'It's true, Gus? You're going to do the dirty on Tosh? You've been talking to knobheads in the west who're offering a sweeter deal?'

'I didn't know–'

'Didn't know I was Tosh's supplier? Who the fuck do you think it was set you up with him back in 2009? Saved you and Wallace running up and down the A1?'

'We were put on to him by a guy called Stuart Grant. A man in his sixties, getting out of the game, retiring to Spain.'

'Any ideas who suggested Grant connect you with Macintosh?'

McMahon said nothing, but his eyes never left Levy.

'Dawning on you now, is it? And you're getting ready to give us the bum's rush?'

'I… I didn't know you were Tosh's supplier, Lionel. It was only business. I was offered 10k a kilo less.'

'And you were throwing us over for that? After all we've done for you? Saving you and that scrote Wallace a fortune in petrol money, not to mention the time wasted barrelling up and down the motorway? I'd call that ungrateful in the extreme.' He turned to the man behind him. 'What do you think, Baz? Sound ungrateful to you?'

The man nodded and answered sonorously, 'Very ungrateful, boss.'

Levy's eyes went to the man sitting alongside. 'What kind of punishment do you think that sort of an insult calls for, Andy?'

Baz's big mate shifted in his seat and the springs protested audibly. 'I'd say it merits a debollocking, boss.'

Levy turned back and faced McMahon. 'You know what a debollocking is, Gus?'

McMahon had begun to sweat. 'I'm sorry, Lionel,' he protested. 'Like I say, I didn't know it was you.'

'You haven't answered the question, bonny lad. I asked you if you knew what a debollocking was.'

McMahon swallowed. 'No.'

Levy pulled back his jacket, took a Beretta automatic from a leather shoulder holder, and thrust it between McMahon's legs.

McMahon felt the muzzle of the pistol press against his testicles and heard an distinct *click* as Levy prised off the safety.

'This automatic's got a hair trigger, Gus,' Levy said. 'Slight pressure is all that's needed to send a bullet blasting into your balls. Now, I'm going to ask a question, and if I don't hear the answer I want, the next thing that happens is you become a eunuch. Oh, and I should warn you; it's a *very* painful business. The question is: are you going to continue with Macintosh?'

McMahon felt his bowels loosen. '*Um-huh.*'

'I need to hear you say it clearly, Gus.'

'Yeah,' McMahon said. 'I'm going to stay with Macintosh.'

'No more meetings with your pals in the west?'

McMahon shook his head vigorously. 'No more meetings.'

Levy removed the weapon from McMahon's crotch, thumbed on the safety catch, and returned it to its holster. 'We'll hold you to your word, Gus,' Levy said. 'Just a whisper of anything different…'

McMahon emitted a huge sigh of relief. 'You've my word. I'll keep it.'

'Good,' Levy said and motioned towards the glove box. 'We were watching the lad in the Mondeo. Just made a deposit, did he?'

McMahon nodded.

'How much?'

'Almost forty-four grand.'

Levy undid the catch and extracted the package. 'Okay,' he said. 'You know, by rights we should have subjected you to a little pain.' He turned to his cohorts. 'That right, lads?'

'That's right, boss,' the pair chorused.

Levy pointed to the pistol at his shoulder. 'On this occasion, though, I think feeling the business end of the gun at your genitals has had an effect: maybe even to the extent of your needing fresh underwear.' He tossed the package over his shoulder and the man called Baz caught it. 'However, we can't let this infraction go completely unpunished. You understand that, don't you, Gus?'

'Forty-four grand's a lot, Lionel,' McMahon protested.

'Indeed,' Levy said. 'Serious money.' A pause. 'But what you and your buddy intended was potentially very serious, too – for us, that is. So I think I'm justified in administering a serious fine, don't you?'

'But that's a quarter of a week's takings.'

Levy nodded over his shoulder. 'Okay, suppose I ask Baz to take only 10k from the envelope, return the rest to you. He and Andy will carry out a little chastisement in exchange for the remainder. I should warn you, though, both my lads are past masters in the art. Might leave you incapacitated for a week or two.'

'Okay… you can take the money,' McMahon replied through dry lips.

Levy smiled. 'A wise choice, bonny lad,' he said. 'A wise choice.'

He closed the glove box and added, 'Now, Gus, there's one other thing I hope you can help us with – Wallace. You know where he is?'

McMahon shook his head. 'Likely to be working his territory somewhere.' He glanced at his watch. 'It's half-five. He might even be at home.'

'No, he isn't,' Levy said. 'We talked to his neighbours. Told us he comes and goes at all hours. Not today, though. Nobody's seen him since early this morning. We've toured all of his haunts too.'

'Afraid I can't help you, Lionel. You're probably aware I've little to do with him.'

'Aye. Tosh told us about bad blood between you – the shooting of your lad. What was that about?'

'One of Wallace's clients moved house; from his territory into mine. Nice bungalow; professional type. Wallace continued to supply him. I instructed my guy to poach a few punters in nearby Oxgangs, his patch. Wallace took exception.'

'Did he do the shooting?'

McMahon shrugged. 'Wouldn't be surprised.'

'Bloody idiot,' Levy said. 'Not good for business. What happened with the cops?'

'I had one visit me at home. Narc Squad, name of Paterson.'

'Oh?'

'Aye, tried it on. Said I'd called Smeaton on the day he was shot. I knew immediately it was a load of flannel. I never call my guys. Only communication they get from me is a text message, coded. Let's them know where to meet me. Like with Jenkins here today; I never choose the same place twice in a row.'

'So how'd it end up?'

'He buggered off. Like I say, it was flannel. The guy was fishing, trying to catch me off guard.'

'Hmm,' Levy said. 'Tosh told me he had a couple of visits, too – DI called Knox. Similar spiel. Said they'd been tracing calls. How he learned about you and Wallace.'

McMahon said nothing, and Levy remained silent for a long moment, deep in thought.

'Okay, Gus,' he said finally. 'I'll have another word with Tosh. See if he can give me a clue as to Wallace's whereabouts. If you've any ideas in the meantime, let me know... we're at the Jury's Inn, and won't be leaving Edinburgh till we find that bastard.'

Chapter Eighteen

Sandrine Cudlipp was a freckle-faced redhead, slightly smaller than Ryan. When she admitted Knox and Fulton to their dorm, Ryan was sitting on her bed, reading a magazine. She looked up as the detectives entered, gave a weak smile, and returned to her reading.

'I didn't know about Clare,' Cudlipp said. 'Last time I saw her was on Monday morning. My uncle John died at the beginning of last week after a long battle with cancer. We're a very close family. I had to go home for the funeral.'

'I understand,' Knox said. 'And we're sorry to call so late. It's just that we wanted to speak to everyone who knew Clare.'

'It's okay,' Cudlipp said. She paused for a moment, then added, 'Rebecca told me you were asking about my vitamins?'

'Vitamin C,' Knox said. 'Ms Ryan told us you take it?'

'I do, yes.' She walked over to her bedside table. 'I forgot to take them with me when I went back home.' She picked up the two bottles that lay there, and added, 'That's funny.'

'What is?' Knox asked.

'There's a full bottle and a completely empty one. I could have sworn I had a few tablets in the second bottle.'

Ryan laid aside her magazine. 'Oh, that's my fault,' she said. 'I borrowed one of your magazines from the table and the bottle fell to the floor. The cap came loose and what tablets were left spilled out. I threw them away and washed out the bottle.'

Knox and Fulton exchanged glances.

'When you spoke to DS Fulton, Ms Ryan,' Knox said, 'you told him you don't share Ms Tomkins' interest in jogging – is that true?'

Ryan gave Knox a diffident look. 'Ye-es. I cycle a lot, but never jog.'

Knox pointed to a pair of Reeboks under her bed. 'Are those yours?'

Ryan frowned. 'Yes.'

Knox nodded and gestured to the empty vitamin C bottle Cudlipp was holding. 'You know, Ms Ryan, modern forensics is quite advanced. We know for a fact that the soil on Fraser McCauley's trainers was contaminated by minute quantities of vitamin C. Vitamin C which I believe came from that bottle.' Knox paused, then added, 'Incidentally, the fact that you washed it doesn't mean our specialists can't still find traces of soil.'

Ryan appeared ashen, but said nothing.

Knox indicated her Reeboks. 'I'm going to take possession of those trainers, too, and submit them for analysis. I believe you've been lying to us.'

Tears began streaming down Ryan's cheeks. 'I *was* there,' she sobbed. 'I told her not to. She wouldn't listen.'

'Told who not to?' Knox asked. 'Who wouldn't listen?'

'My friend, Louise.'

'Who's Louise?' Knox asked. He glanced at Cudlipp, who gave him a baffled look and shrugged.

'Louise Jardine,' Ryan said. 'You don't know her, Sandrine. She's a childhood friend, arrived on Monday, after you left. I last saw her when we were thirteen.'

'Where is she now?' Knox asked.

'Somewhere in the city, I think. I'm not sure where.' Ryan dabbed her eyes with a tissue and continued, 'I invited her into the dorm and we began discussing things we got up to as kids. Then she asked about relationships, who I was seeing at the campus, that sort of thing.'

'And?'

'I told her I'd only been on one date.'

'With who?'

'David Martin. I told her I'd quite a crush on him. She was glad for me, she said, as when we were younger I was shy where boys were concerned. I told her it was only one date, not a relationship. She asked why I hadn't continued seeing him. I told her I didn't know why, he'd since begun dating Clare. She flew into a rage, became quite irrational. Claimed I hadn't changed, wasn't assertive enough. Said I let others walk over me, that I'd allowed Clare to entice David away.'

'What happened then?' Knox asked.

'I changed the subject, and eventually she calmed down. We began talking about other things until quite late. She asked if she could stay over, and I agreed. Next morning she was up early. Told me she'd seen Clare heading to Holyrood Park in her running gear. I said it was something Clare did most mornings. She became angry again, insisting I was a fool for letting her come between me and David. She said she was going to follow and give Clare a piece of her mind. I tried to dissuade her, but Louise is headstrong – she wouldn't listen. She went after Clare and I followed; all the while trying to make her see reason.'

'But by the time you got to the park it would have been thick with fog,' Fulton said. 'How did you know where Ms Tomkins was headed?'

'Louise asked the same question,' Ryan said. 'I told her she normally followed a track on the other side of the cliffs.'

'So, you both caught up with her,' Knox said. 'What happened then?'

'Oh, no, we didn't *both* catch up with her,' Ryan said. 'I suffer from acrophobia, I was terrified of going near the cliff edge. Louise carried on by herself.'

'While you waited?'

'Yes.'

'How long was she gone?'

'I'm not sure, maybe five or ten minutes.'

'Did you hear or see anything while you were waiting?'

'No.'

'What did she say when she returned?'

'Not much.'

'She admitted to killing Clare?'

'No.'

'Did she say anything about taking the soil sample?'

'I told her I suspected she'd taken it, but she never actually admitted doing so.'

'Hmm,' Knox said. 'When I asked if you knew where Louise was, you said somewhere in town. Surely she must have told you where she's staying.'

'I… I honestly couldn't say.'

'Couldn't say – or wouldn't say?'

Ryan bit her lip. 'I'm sorry. I can't help you.'

'Okay,' Knox said. 'Rebecca Ryan, I'm arresting you under section 1 of the Criminal Justice Scotland Act 2016, on a charge of being an accessory to murder. You don't have to say anything now, but will be able to do so at the police station in the presence of a solicitor of your choice.'

* * *

Knox arrived at the office the next morning and was intercepted by the duty desk sergeant, Charlie Roker. 'Helluva night with the Ryan girl,' he said. 'Screaming hysterically one minute, babbling a lot of incoherent nonsense the next.'

'The MO was called?'

'Yes. Unfortunately, Dr Haigh isn't on nights this week. We got his locum, a young guy called Aspinall.'

'He saw her?'

'Yes. I couple of officers had to subdue her while he administered a sedative. He's of the opinion Dr Haigh should see her. Aspinall's going to ask him to come in as soon as he comes on duty.'

'How is she now?'

'Quiet. We've been carrying out a twenty-minute cell check since Dr Aspinall left.'

'Okay, Charlie. I'll be in the office if Haigh wants to see me.'

'Righto, boss.'

Knox entered the office and saw his team were already at their desks.

'I heard Ryan was a bit restless in the night,' Fulton said. 'Had to be sedated.'

'Yes,' Knox confirmed. 'Charlie just told me.' Knox indicated a computer terminal. 'Any luck with Ryan's next of kin?'

'Aye,' Fulton said, nodding to Hathaway. 'Mark phoned Pollock Hall's admin first thing. It appears Ryan was fostered.' He glanced at Hathaway. 'Mark?'

'Aye, boss,' Hathaway confirmed. 'Their secretary just sent me an email. Gives her next of kin as Mr Kenneth Lowrie and his wife Grace.' He studied the computer screen and added, 'Number 41 Richmond Green, Kelso.'

'Phone number?'

'Aye, we have it.'

Knox nodded to McCann. 'You want to speak to them, Arlene?'

McCann smiled. 'Bad news sounds better coming from a woman, huh, boss?'

'Something like that.'

McCann placed her telephone on speaker and dialled the number, which rang three times and a woman answered, 'Hello?'

'Hi, Mrs Grace Lowrie?'

'Yes.'

'This is Detective Sergeant Arlene McCann, Edinburgh police. I'm phoning to ask if you can confirm you're the foster parent of Rebecca Ryan, a student at Heriot-Watt University, currently residing at the Pollock Hall Campus?'

'I am, yes.' Lowrie's voice suddenly sounded tremulous. 'Has anything happened to her?'

'She's okay, Mrs Lowrie,' McCann said. 'She's in custody at Gayfield Square Police Station.'

'In custody? Why?'

'A girl called Clare Tomkins was murdered on Tuesday morning. We've reason to believe Rebecca was complicit in her death.'

'Surely not.'

'I'm afraid so.'

'What is she charged with?'

'Accessory to murder.'

'Accessory?' Lowrie said. 'That means she aided the person who murdered the girl, doesn't it?'

'Yes, ma'am,' McCann said. 'It does.'

'Who was it?'

'A Ms Louise Jardine is suspected. You know her?'

'No. No, I don't think so.'

'Okay. I wonder if you'd help me with some background details, Mrs Lowrie,' McCann said. 'When did you foster Rebecca?'

'When she was thirteen. We were on the foster register at the time and were contacted by social services.'

'Oh?' McCann said. 'What were the circumstances?'

'Her mother was a drug addict and her father subjected her to sexual abuse. After her mother took an overdose and died, a neighbour contacted the authorities and she was taken into care. She came to us in 2013.' Mrs Lowrie paused. 'Look, this accessory charge – there couldn't have been some mistake? I can't believe Rebecca would allow herself to get mixed up in murder.'

'As I told you, Mrs Lowrie,' McCann said, 'the girl suspected hasn't been found yet, so we don't have a complete picture. Rebecca will remain in custody until we're able to discover the extent of her involvement. She may be allowed bail at some point after that. Do you have a solicitor?'

'Yes, my husband does.'

'It might be helpful if you could have them contact us.'

'Can we see her?'

'Of course. Ring us back and let us know when you can come in. We'll make the necessary arrangements.'

* * *

'A couple of days before Tate hanged himself, I heard that one of the younger cons got a phone call,' Malachy was saying.

DI Madden and DS Gray were seated opposite him in one of Saughton Prison's interview rooms and the inmate was answering their questions.

'On a mobile, which does the rounds,' Malachy continued. 'Costs a premium, but a lot easier than waiting to use your card on one of the landlines.'

'Which inmate, do you know?' Madden asked.

'Pete Gifford, one of the two who got into a fight with Tate in the yard.'

'Any idea who the caller was?' Gray said.

Malachy shook his head. 'Sorry, can't help you there.'

'Do you remember an inmate called Moran?' Madden asked.

'Aye, the bodybuilder,' Malachy said. 'He was called that because he was never out of the gym. Liked pumping weights.'

'Do you think the call might have been from him?'

'Might've. I know Gifford was one of Moran's circle of cronies while he was here.'

'The man with him on the day of the fight,' Gray asked, 'you know who it was?'

'Ted Curtis. Thick as thieves, the pair of them.' Malachy suddenly burst out laughing. 'Thick as thieves. Funny, eh?'

'Why do you think they went after Tate?' Gray said.

'Gifford took a downer on him because he'd a relative who was raped.'

'An aunt?'

'Yeah.'

'And Curtis?'

'His sister's husband was a real bastard—' He paused and locked Gray in the eye. 'Pardon my French, Miss. He was always drunk; gave his wife a good few hidings. Then one weekend he went over the score and stabbed her. Luckily, she survived. He copped a sentence of two years. Ended up in Peterhead's VPU wing. Just as well; he'd have been singled out for special attention otherwise, as happened to Tate here.'

'The attack on Tate,' Madden said, 'it took place soon after Gifford received the phone call?'

Malachy's brow furrowed and he glanced at the ceiling. 'You know, come to think of it, it did,' he replied. 'A day or two later, in fact.'

'Do you know if Tate was targeted at any other time?'

'Apart from in the yard?'

'Yes.'

Malachy shrugged. 'Quite a grapevine in here. Doesn't take long to learn what someone's in for. It went around pretty quick that he was a rapist. Only other time I saw Gifford and Curtis near him was in the canteen. Even then, though, he gave them a wide berth.' He paused. 'But there was one occasion...'

'Yes?'

'In the shower block, a couple of weeks back – those of us in the metal shop tend to use it last. I showered and dried off, got dressed, and was leaving when I glanced behind me.'

'Go on,' Madden said.

'I saw Tate dabbing his nose with a towel. Someone must've got to him there – it was bloody.'

Chapter Nineteen

McCann was about to wind up the call when Lowrie said, 'Louise.'

'Pardon?' McCann said.

'Louise – the girl you are looking for,' Lowrie said. 'I just remembered. Rebecca had a friend called Louise just before she came to us. Her name was Louise.'

'Whereabouts was this, Mrs Lowrie?' McCann asked.

'In Hawick, the town Rebecca originally comes from… and, if I'm not mistaken, her surname was Jardine.'

The detectives exchanged glances, and McCann said, 'She was a close friend?'

'Yes,' Lowrie replied. 'Which made what happened all the more devastating.'

'What happened?'

'An accident on Hawick High Street. Louise ran out in front of a lorry and was killed.'

* * *

As McCann ended the call, Knox's mobile rang and he glanced at the screen and saw the caller was DI Madden from West End Police Station. 'We've just finished talking to Malachy,' he said. 'Thought you'd like to know how it went.'

'Aye?' Knox said. 'Anything interesting?'

'Well, you were right to wonder about the incident in the yard – happened not long after Pete Gifford, one of the pair who assaulted Tate, received a phone call.'

'It was from Moran?'

'Malachy isn't sure, but Gifford and Curtis – the other guy in the yard fracas – were friendly with Moran when he was inside.'

'Anything to indicate Tate was being bullied by Gifford and Curtis?'

'Nothing concrete. Malachy told us he stayed well out of their way.'

'Anything else?'

'Yeah. An incident in the shower block. Predates the phone call.'

'What happened?'

'Malachy witnessed Tate leave the showers with a bloody nose. Didn't see who did it.'

Knox thanked Madden, ended the call, and just as he returned the mobile to his pocket, his landline rang.

'Knox?'

'Charlie Roker again, boss. The senior MO, Dr Haigh, has just seen Ryan.'

'Aye?'

'On her way to the Royal Edinburgh at Morningside accompanied by a couple of officers. She's been sectioned.'

* * *

The Royal Edinburgh Psychiatric Hospital was located in Morningside, a middle-class suburb a twenty-minute drive from Gayfield Square. An hour after Roker informed him Ryan had been admitted, Knox had received a call from a Dr Gavin Ross asking to see him, and he and DS McCann were on their way to keep the appointment.

'A bit unexpected, don't you think, boss?' McCann said as they neared their destination.

'Haigh's section order?'

'Uh-huh. Bill told me she seemed fine when you spoke to her last night.'

'She was,' Knox said. 'But apparently the night shift boys had a helluva time – screaming, hysterics, the lot. Had to subdue her while the medic gave her a shot.'

'I wonder what made her react that way?'

'Don't know. But it must've been serious if Haigh decided on sectioning.'

'Hmm,' McCann said. 'I wonder what Ross has to tell us.'

Knox passed a row of shops set back off the road, signalled right, and indicated an entranceway ahead. 'We'll soon find out,' he said.

Knox parked the car and they entered a glass-panelled reception area. There they were directed along a corridor to Ross's office, where he met the detectives and ushered them into an oblong room with a large flat-screen television faced by rows of chairs.

'This room is attached to our assessment suite,' he said. 'Linked by CCTV, which allows junior doctors, therapists and others in the field of psychiatry to monitor methods used to determine the mental health of the individuals assessed.'

He picked up a remote from a stand and switched on the set. 'I wanted you to see this, Inspector, to understand the reasons why Dr Haigh issued Ms Ryan's section order.'

The television came on and gave a wide view a room where a Formica-topped table and a chair at either end were the only objects of furniture.

Ross took a mobile phone from his pocket and called a number. 'You can tell Professor Dott we're ready now,' he said.

He replaced the phone and addressed Knox. 'Professor Alistair Dott is a specialist in these types of cases,' he said.

'I'm not sure I follow,' Knox said. 'What types of cases?'

Ross gave Knox a mystified look. 'Ms Ryan,' he said. 'I thought Dr Haigh told you what he suspected?'

Knox shook his head. 'No, I didn't see Dr Haigh. All we were told was that she'd been sectioned. An hour after that I received your phone call.'

'Oh, I see,' Ross said. As he spoke, Knox's attention was taken by the monitor, which showed two male nurses escorting Ryan into the assessment room. One of the nurses indicated a chair nearest the door and Ryan took a seat. Both nurses then stood by the door and a third man came into the room. He was in late middle age and dressed casually.

Ross gestured to the monitor. 'That's Professor Dott,' he said. 'And if you're wondering why Ms Ryan looks a bit vacant, she's been sedated.'

'You were going to tell us why she was sectioned?'

'Oh, yes,' Ross said. 'The young woman is suffering from DID – dissociative identity disorder, a condition where someone has two or more distinct identities. Usually caused by trauma, particularly in childhood, which we're sure is the case here. According to the social services report, she suffered at the hands of an abusive father and her mother died of a drugs overdose. Both bad enough, but she also had a close friend who was killed in a traffic accident.'

'Louise Jardine?' McCann said.

'Yes. We think Rebecca's way of dealing with the trauma was to take on the personality of Louise, who became her second self, or "alter" as we call them.'

'So she has a split personality?' McCann asked.

'Yes,' Ross agreed. 'Two psyches in one individual, each completely different from the other.'

He nodded to the screen. 'Professor Dott is about to begin,' he said. 'He'll establish rapport with Rebecca first, before attempting a dialogue with her alter.'

Ross turned up the volume, and Knox heard a chair scrape on the tiled floor as Dott moved his seat nearer the table. He placed his arms on the Formica top, clasped his hands together, and smiled. 'Good morning, Rebecca,' he said gently.

Ryan said nothing, her face expressionless.

'Or is it Louise I'm talking to?'

A flicker of recognition as he said the name, and Ryan answered, 'Louise?'

'Yes,' Dott said. 'Your friend – is she with you now?'

Ryan stirred in her seat. 'She did something bad,' she replied, a childlike quality to her voice.

'What did she do that was bad, Rebecca?'

'She… she killed Clare.'

'Clare Tomkins?'

'Yes.'

'Do you want to tell me what happened?' Dott said. 'From the very beginning.'

Tears began streaming down Ryan's face. 'They said she was dead. That she'd been hit by a lorry. But she came back.'

'Louise?'

'Yes.'

'When did she come back?'

'A week after the funeral.'

'What happened?'

'She began to talk to me. Often. Stayed until I was fostered by Mrs Lowrie.'

'What did you talk about?'

'Things.'

'What kind of things?'

Ryan rolled her eyes. 'You know,' she said.

'No, Rebecca, I don't. Why don't you tell me?'

She shrugged. 'Music, make-up… boys.'

'Go on.'

'She always used to chide me for being so shy. Said I lacked confidence.'

'How often did she visit you then?'

'Every few days.'

'Before she visited, how did you feel?'

'I don't know what you mean.'

'Were you happy, or sad?'

'Mostly unhappy.'

'Your mother had died?'

'Yes. And my father did things. Awful things.'

'Louise comforted you?'

'Yes. Made me feel better.'

'What happened after you were fostered by the Lowries? Did she visit you then?'

'Not as often.'

'How often?'

'Every month or so in the beginning.' Ryan took a tissue from inside her sleeve and dabbed her eyes. 'Not much after that.'

'You told Dr Haigh you saw her again this week. When was the last time you saw her before then?'

'I'm not sure.'

'Months? Years?'

'Years, probably.'

'Okay, what happened on Monday?'

'It was Sunday.'

'Pardon?'

'Sunday night. I was on my way to the dorm after I'd been at the café. The other girls left to do some cramming – Fiona and Sofia – they've exams coming up. Anyway, it was just Clare and I who stayed, talking. Then Dave Martin came in and joined us. I didn't stay long after that.'

'Why?'

'Because they were seeing each other. I felt I was intruding.'

'So, you were on your way to Glassel House. What happened then?'

'Louise came back.'

'Did she tell you why?'

'Because she was annoyed. No – angry. Said it was just like when we were back in Hawick. I'd allowed another person to take advantage of me.'

'Clare?'

'Yes. I'd been terribly fond of David, you see. But I'd been too shy to tell him.'

'What did Louise advise?'

'That I speak to Clare, tell her to stop seeing him.'

'How did you respond?'

'I told her it didn't matter. That I was over it, I didn't want to cause trouble.'

'She stayed with you on Sunday?'

'No, she went away then. Didn't come back until Monday afternoon, after Sandrine had returned to Leicester.'

'Sandrine, she's your room-mate?'

'Yes.'

'So, Louise returned on Monday. What did she say?'

'That I should definitely have a word with Clare, and if I didn't, she would.'

'I see,' Dott said. 'Carry on.'

'I successfully managed to steer her off the subject, and thought she'd forgotten about it – until Tuesday morning. She rose early, spotted Clare leaving for her morning jog, and insisted on going after her. I tried to talk her out of it, but she wouldn't listen.'

'You followed her to Holyrood Park?'

'Yes. To a track near the top of the cliffs. Clare was in the habit of using it, as she liked to take photographs of the Edinburgh skyline from there.'

'You continued along the cliff path?'

'Yes. But as we approached it got quite misty. By the time we arrived the fog was really quite thick. I'm afraid of heights. I was worried about going near the edge and falling. I told Louise I couldn't go further.'

'What did she say?'

Ryan was silent for a long moment, then suddenly stiffened, sat bolt upright in the chair, and a different look came over her. She began speaking, but his time her voice had a deeper timbre.

'I told her to stay where she was if she was frightened. That I'd go on alone.'

Dott studied Ryan closely, and nodded slowly. 'I'm speaking to Louise now,' he said. 'Is that correct?'

'Yes.'

'Okay. Will you continue from when you left Rebecca?'

'I carried on. The fog had thickened, but it didn't take long to find Clare. She was standing at the topmost part of the cliffs, taking a picture with her iPhone.'

'Did you say anything?'

'No.'

'You were angry?'

'Seething. She'd taken advantage of my closest friend. A girl she knew to be quiet and shy; someone who abhorred confrontation. Flaunted herself at the boy Becky adored and enticed him away. Of course I was angry. My friend is a sweet, kind soul who's suffered greatly. Lost her mother at thirteen. Endured endless abuse from a pervert of a father. But that didn't bother Clare. She betrayed a friendship, hijacked David's affections without a second thought. And there she was, snapping photos without a care in the world.'

'She spoke to you?' Dott asked.

Louise tossed back her head. 'I didn't give the bitch time to. I was determined to punish her for her callousness – I gave her a good thumping.'

'But surely you realised she was at the edge of a precipice, in danger of falling,' Dott said. 'You pursued her until she slipped and fell?'

'She'd broken my best friend's heart,' Louise replied. 'I forced her to break her neck.'

Chapter Twenty

Professor Dott concluded the interview and the two nurses escorted Ryan from the room. Dr Ross muted the sound and turned to Knox. 'Clare Tomkins was murdered by Ryan while the Louise part of her personality was dominant,' he said. 'Acting in what she thought were her friend's best interests. The sad part about it, of course, is that her condition wasn't picked up earlier. You spoke to Mrs Lowrie – she hadn't noticed anything in the time Rebecca was with her?'

'Apart from the fact that at thirteen her mother died and her father was abusive, no,' Knox said. 'And the death of the real Louise around the same time.'

'Yes,' Ross replied. 'She said during the consultation she hadn't channelled her alter much in recent years.' He paused. 'Seeing her ex-boyfriend in the café with Clare was most likely the catalyst. It triggered the reappearance of the more assertive Louise.'

Knox nodded. 'You'll make a recording of Professor Dott's interview with Ms Ryan available to us?'

'Of course,' Ross said. 'She'll be charged with Clare Tomkins murder?'

'I've only limited experience with cases of this nature,' Knox said. 'But it'll be referred to the procurator fiscal, and a panel of medical professionals – including Professor Dott, no doubt – will be consulted. A hearing held in bar of trial is likely and she'll be committed to care of the state under section 174 of the Criminal Procedure Act. What happens after that will be determined by how she responds to treatment. I'm inclined to think she'll be institutionalised for a while.'

* * *

Knox and McCann were climbing the stairs to the office at Gayfield Square when his mobile rang. He checked its screen and didn't recognise the number.

'Knox?' he said.

'You're Detective Inspector Knox?' a man asked.

'Yes. Who's speaking?'

'Sandy Purvis, 9 Kaimes Green Crescent. We spoke on Tuesday, you left me a card.'

Knox covered the mouthpiece and turned to McCann. 'Carry on,' he said. 'I'll catch you up.' Then to Purvis, 'Yes, Mr Purvis. How can I help?'

'I hope to help *you*,' Purvis said. 'It's to do with that lad you asked about; the one with the red baseball hat?'

'Oh,' Knox said. 'Right.'

'I found out who he is.'

'Really?'

'Aye,' Purvis said. 'The teenager who delivers the *Evening News*, calls on a Friday to collect his money, asked how I was keeping. We got talking and I told him about the lad with the phone. Said you were looking for him. The lad knew him, told me where he stays.'

'Go on,' Knox said.

'His name is Tommy Kennedy. Lives in a flat at 25/8 Kaimes Green Court.'

Knox thanked Purvis, ended the call, and entered the office and was intercepted by Fulton. 'DCS Steele called when you were at Morningside, boss,' Fulton said. 'Wants you to ring him ASAP.'

'He's in the city?' Knox asked.

'At St Leonards, I think.'

Knox turned to McCann, who came in from the vending machine with two coffees and handed him one. 'Ta, Arlene,' he said, 'bet you a tenner his plans have gone awry.'

She nodded. 'Not sure that's a bet I'd take you up on, boss.'

Knox put his telephone on speaker, dialled Steele's number, and a moment later heard the DCS. 'Steele?'

'DI Knox, sir. Returning your call.'

'Ah, yes, Knox. This Lionel fellow and Macintosh. Things aren't quite panning out as we expected.'

Knox glanced at McCann, who rolled her eyes.

'Wallace,' Steele continued, 'seems to have disappeared.'

'Sir?'

A short silence. 'Perhaps I'd better bring you up to speed on what's taken place since we spoke last. By the way, before I start, let me tell you that I'm in our requisitioned office in St Leonards, and that both DS Lyall and DS Hammond are in the room with me. Is DS McCann at your end?'

'Yes, sir.'

'Good, then we'll make this a conference call. First, McMahon. DS Lyall followed him to a meeting with one of his pushers at the car park of Morrisons supermarket in Gilmerton Road. Just before eight last night.

'Things started well. We latched on to Lionel and two of his cohorts – DS Hammond's photographs with a telephoto lens scored a hit with Northumbria Police's facial recognition software. The men were subsequently identified as Andrew Nevins and Basil Musgrave, both known felons. Lionel, by the way, was pegged as Lionel Levy, aka Stephen Goldman. The vehicles with them – a

Land Rover Discovery and Mitsubishi Shogun – were on false plates.

'Our Geordie friends spoke to McMahon for a while, during which time DS Lyall had the impression he was under a fair degree of duress. No doubt being persuaded that leaving Macintosh wasn't a good idea.' A pause. 'Over to you, Keith.'

'I kept a bit of distance between us as we entered Morrisons,' Lyall said. 'There's a bit of a bend as you enter and I saw him park behind a Mondeo halfway between the entrance and the supermarket itself. At first I didn't notice the Land Rover and Mitsubishi – I was looking for the best vantage point to watch McMahon when I saw them cruise into bays either side of the central row where the Audi and Mondeo were parked. I found a space further over and waited. The Mondeo guy didn't waste any time – a couple of minutes and he was gone.

'McMahon had just started his engine when the Land Rover and Mitsubishi moved swiftly and blocked him. The two big lads – Nevins and Musgrave – left the Mitsubishi and got in the back, Levy exited the Rover and jumped into the front. They'd a fairly long talk – or I should say Levy did, as he was doing most of the talking. They stayed around ten minutes.'

'It was DS Hammond who spotted them earlier in the day,' Steele said, 'when Northumbria Police tipped us off he'd been seen driving north. Steve?'

'Yes, sir,' Hammond confirmed. 'Picked them up at the Old Craighall interchange and followed them along the bypass to the Hermiston Gait cut-off. They headed directly for Broomhall Grove, parked near Wallace's house, and waited a couple of hours. Must've became impatient, because when he didn't show, Levy left the Land Rover and went to the houses nearby, presumably asking neighbours if they'd seen him. The answer obviously was negative, as he'd a face like thunder when he returned to the Rover.'

'We used other unmarked cars to keep them in sight,' Steele said. 'They returned to the city centre, booked into the Jury's Inn hotel in Jeffrey Street, where they remained until they left to catch up with McMahon.'

'So, what happened to Wallace?' Knox asked.

'The sixty-four thousand dollar question,' Steele said. 'DI Paterson took over DS Hammond's surveillance yesterday, followed Wallace to a supermarket in Granton, where he met a pusher. Paterson tailed him all the way to Corstorphine and was caught in heavy traffic in St John's Road, where he was cut out by two fire engines on an emergency call. When the tenders had passed, Wallace had disappeared.'

'He hadn't been on his way to Broomhall?' Knox asked.

'No,' Steele replied. 'Paterson told me it was the first place he looked. No sign.'

'And Lionel and his crew,' Knox said, 'they're still in Edinburgh?'

'Yes. It would appear they're searching for him, too.'

Steele said nothing for a long moment. 'Not too worry, though,' he continued. 'Curtailment of drugs is our *raison d'être*. Northumbria Police in Newcastle got back to me. I spoke to the man heading their narcotics division, DCS Alan Hyde. He said they've had their eye on Levy for some time, and want to work with us.

'Naturally, I agreed. They've been watching his place in Sunderland, a farm near a village called Cleadon. It's believed he's bringing drugs into the country and stashing them there. No cast-iron evidence yet, which they need before mounting a raid.

'Levy's preoccupation with Macintosh, though, has been helpful: his trip to Edinburgh has allowed their surveillance team to get close, and they're hopeful of nailing him when he returns. Of course I'd like to be sure of where Macintosh is caching his drugs, too. Anyway, we've no option but to sit on it for the moment. See how this thing with Wallace develops.'

'I've a bit of news that might help us there, sir,' Knox said.

'To do with Wallace?' Steele said.

'In a way, yes. I received a call from Mr Purvis, the ex-bus driver who was injured when Smeaton was murdered.'

'Go on.'

'Before the killer struck, a man kept watch to make sure Smeaton was in a vulnerable position. Mr Purvis found out who that man is.'

'He gave you a name, an address?'

'Yes, sir, a lad called Kennedy, lives in the same area. With your permission I'd like to see him, make the arrest.'

'Of course, Knox. Excellent work. Keep me informed, will you?'

'Sir.'

* * *

Lionel Levy was sitting drinking coffee together with Musgrave and Nevins in the lounge of the Jury's Inn when a waiter approached their table. 'Mr Levy?' he said.

'Yes?' Levy replied.

'Telephone call for you at reception, sir.'

Levy gave a look of curiosity. 'Really?'

'Yes, sir,' the man replied.

Levy rose, walked through to reception, and the girl behind the desk looked up and indicated a booth opposite.

'In there, sir,' she said. 'I'll switch your call through.'

Levy entered the booth, closed the door, and picked up the handset. 'Hello?'

'Lionel? Gus McMahon. I just remembered Wallace has a flat in Leith. He was involved with a barmaid last year, bought it so he could meet her without his wife knowing. Before she found out and skedaddled, that is.'

'Where in Leith?' Levy asked.

'175d Manderston Street.'

'You're sure he still has the flat?'

'I think so. He was seeing the girl up until a couple of months ago, when his wife left him.'

'Right, Gus. If this info proves kosher, you've earned yourself a couple of Brownie points.'

Levy went back to the lounge and buttonholed the waiter. 'I need a taxi,' he said. 'But I don't want to leave by the front entrance. You've a back door?'

'Aye, sir. There's a side entrance, leads to North Gray's Close. You can walk up to the High Street. There's a taxi rank opposite.'

Levy's brow furrowed. 'Close?'

'Scottish name for an alleyway, sir. Like I say, it leads to the High Street.'

Levy pressed a twenty-pound note into the man's hand. 'Right,' he said. 'Me and my mates'll be out for a while. Keep that to yourself, you understand?'

The waiter glanced at the note and broke into a broad smile. 'Perfectly, sir.'

Chapter Twenty-one

Levy had the taxi driver drop them off at the corner of Manderston Street and Easter Road, and they walked the short distance to 175, a new-build block of flats a third of the way along the street.

Levy studied the occupants listed next to the buzzers at the entrance, and saw Wallace's flat was on the second floor.

'Don't want to let him know we're here till we're outside his door,' Levy said.

'I could buzz someone,' Musgrave said. 'Pretend I'm a courier leaving a parcel.'

The door opened at that moment and an elderly man exited with a Highland terrier on a leash. Levy smiled at him and said, 'Nice day,' and caught the door before it closed.

The man nodded and carried on with the dog in his wake.

'Good idea, Baz,' Levy said. 'But this way is better.'

The trio ascended the stairs and pressed a buzzer outside 175d, and a moment later Wallace answered in a dressing gown.

Musgrave elbowed his way into the hallway and Nevins and Levy followed.

'What the hell's going on?' Wallace said.

As his companions strong-armed Wallace into the living room, Levy glanced around. 'Paying a little social call, Shug,' he said. 'Nice pad, by the way.'

'Do I know you?' Wallace said.

'Aye. You could say we've crossed paths on more than one occasion,' Levy replied. 'As to what's going on, Shug, I think that's a question only you can answer.'

'You know Macintosh?' Wallace asked.

'Getting warmer, Shug. Getting warmer.'

'You're his supplier?'

'I can see you're having difficulty placing me, Shug,' Levy said. 'So I'll give you a little clue: Danny Lawson.'

Wallace gave a look of comprehension as it suddenly clicked into place: Lionel Levy, Lawson's right-hand man. He looked markedly different from when he'd last seen him; balding, slimmer, and sporting a thin moustache.

'You're Lionel,' Wallace said. 'Lionel Levy.'

'Top o' the class, bonny lad,' Levy said. He nodded to Musgrave and Nevins. 'And these are me mates, Baz and Andy.' A pause. 'Like me, Shug, they're none too pleased at the run-around you've given us. But then, I dinna think you were all that keen on being found. Am I right, bonny lad?'

A jumble of thoughts raced through Wallace's mind. Paterson had told him Macintosh had rumbled they were planning a move, which was why he'd contacted Levy.

Had the Geordie sussed that the dealers were phoney, too? That they were in fact undercover cops? Which begged the question – did Levy know Paterson had got to him, that the crooked DI had him in his pocket? More importantly, was Levy aware the police were planning to take down his entire operation?

If that were true, Levy and his henchmen were here for only one reason – they were planning to kill him. He felt panic rise in his throat, yet forced himself to stay calm.

Think.

The Glock automatic! It lay in the top drawer of the drinks cabinet – here, in the living room.

His mind continued to race. They, too, were bound to be armed. Surely not all three, though?

No, likely only one – and that would be Levy.

But *did* he know about the sting? Wallace couldn't be sure. Maybe he was simply here at Macintosh's behest, aggrieved he and McMahon were changing suppliers. Better to play along, see what transpired. If it all went south… well, his pistol was only a couple of feet away; cocked and ready.

'I've been seeing another woman and my wife's been giving me grief,' he said. 'Calling at the house in Broomhall, sometimes with her mother in tow. Decided to move here for a week or two. Until my lawyer sorts it out.'

'Aye, dangerous thing, playing away from home,' Levy said. He looked at the men with him and gave a little wink. 'In love or in business, eh, lads?'

As his companions laughed, Levy's expression changed – he gave Wallace a cold, hard stare. 'But it wasn't just your missus you were planning on leaving, was it Shug?'

'Tosh was planning to sell me out to the cops,' Wallace protested. 'After a DI called Knox had a talk with him, he almost said as much.'

'Away, man,' Levy said. 'You're talking bollocks.'

'After Smeaton's death he panicked, accused me of putting the entire operation at risk. He was planning to grass me up.'

'You're lying,' Levy said. 'You were in the middle of a turf war with McMahon. When Smeaton was shot, he told you to cool it. Sort out your differences. Shooting the lad was bad for business, called unnecessary attention from the cops – a sentiment I happen to agree with. No, Tosh wasn't going to sell you out. There was only one thing behind your intention to bugger off: greed, pure and simple.'

Levy picked up a filigree silver cigarette box from a nearby coffee table, examined it, and put it down again.

'You can flannel all you like, bonny lad, but the truth is plain to see. You were jumping ship because your Glaswegian pals were offering a better deal. 10k a kilo less that you were paying Tosh. McMahon told us. Greed, Shug,' Levy continued. 'The same greed that led you to breach the agreement Tosh had arranged between you and Gus over territory. Greed which saw you leave your own patch because one of your punters moved into his. When he retaliated, you shot his pusher. By the way, *you* did the shooting, didn't you, Shug? Not someone else, as you told Tosh?'

'The client in Swanston spent 3–5k a week,' Wallace said. 'What was I supposed to do – kiss it goodbye because he moved a couple of streets away?' Wallace shook his head. 'McMahon had his guy move into Oxgangs, sell to *dozens* of my punters. Was that fair? No. When I killed Smeaton I was making a statement.'

'Aye, bonny lad, you were making a statement all right. Couldn't have been more effective if you'd used a loudhailer. Brought the entire narc squad down on our heads.' A pause. 'Like I say, a bloody dangerous thing to do.'

'What else could I have done? I couldn't let him away with it.'

Levy studied Wallace for a long moment. 'No, I suppose not. Any more than we can let you away with what you've done to us.'

'What do you mean?'

'The trouble you've put us to,' Levy replied. 'See, Shug, you've got to be able to trust people. Make a deal with someone, you expect that deal to be honoured. One party becomes unreliable, what do you do? The answer's obvious – find a new partner. Which'll happen in your case. McMahon is going to take over your operation, effective immediately. He'll service both south-east and south-west Edinburgh.'

As Levy spoke, he took his Beretta from his shoulder holster and levelled it at Wallace. 'Which means you're a wee bit redundant.'

Wallace rushed to the drinks cabinet, opened the drawer and grabbed the Glock, which he attempted to bring to bear. He'd succeeded in closing his finger on the trigger when a round from Levy's pistol smashed into his chest. He dropped to the floor, where he lay spread-eagled.

Levy fired again into Wallace's supine body, unscrewed a suppressor from the muzzle, and nodded to his companions. 'It was just a guess about Smeaton,' he said. 'But I was right. Wallace was the shooter.'

* * *

Knox and McCann were approaching the junction of Liberton Brae and Lasswade Road when the traffic lights changed to amber, then red. Now on the southern outskirts of the city, they were only a couple of miles from their destination – Tommy Kennedy's flat at Kaimes Green Court.

As Knox came to a stop, a green Toyota Proace van cruised to a halt on his nearside, and positioned for a left turn into Lasswade Road.

McCann glanced at the vehicle, and saw it was lettered: *Rosalind's – Flowers for Every Occasion*. She continued her appraisal for several moments, then suddenly nudged Knox's elbow. 'Look, boss.'

'What?' Knox replied.

'The flower van alongside – small lettering on the panel near the offside rear wheel.'

Knox looked over and saw *B. Macintosh Prop. Registered Office, 581 St John's Road.*

'581 St John's Road,' McCann continued, 'that's his fruit shop, isn't it?'

'You're right,' Knox said. 'Appears he omitted to tell us he'd another outlet.'

McCann flicked on her iPhone, tapped the Google icon, and entered *Rosalind's Flower Shop* into the search box.

She studied the results and nodded to the van. 'There's two registered with that name. One at 55 Lasswade Drive, the other at 76 Colinton Mains Broadway.'

'The website doesn't give the proprietor's name?' Knox asked.

'No, just the shops.'

'Hmm,' Knox said. 'Curious. One in south-east Edinburgh, the other south-west.'

Moments later the lights changed and the van turned into Lasswade Road and Knox continued on to Liberton Brae.

'Same areas worked by McMahon and Wallace,' McCann said.

'Aye,' Knox agreed. 'Quite a coincidence.'

'You think that's how he's doing it – distributing drugs via the flower shops?'

Knox dipped his head in affirmation. 'Never mentioned them when he spoke to us at Gillespie Road,' he said. 'Though he was keen to boast about his three fruit shops.'

'Even offered to show us the books,' McCann said.

'Yeah.' Knox placed his iPhone on the dashboard and keyed in a number. 'I'll give the lads a ring, ask them to take a look.'

Seconds later Fulton's voice came over the speakers. 'Boss?'

'Bill,' Knox said. 'You and Mark still in the office?'

'Aye,' Fulton said. 'Finishing up paperwork on the Tomkins case. Thinking of going over to The Windsor afterwards for a bit of nosh.'

'Be obliged if you'd take lunch on the hoof today, Bill.'

'Something's come up?'

'Macintosh. Arlene and I think we've discovered how he's distributing the drugs.'

'Aye?'

'Uh-huh. Just clocked a van with his name on it; he's the owner of two flower shops he's kept quiet about – one at Lasswade Drive, the other at Colinton Mains Broadway.'

'You want us to organise a raid?'

'No, Bill. Something a little more subtle – for now. I'd like you and Mark to watch both shops for few hours. See who's coming and going.'

'You mean his distributors?' Fulton said. 'I thought Wallace had disappeared?'

'Aye, so it would seem. But there's always Macintosh and his sidekick Moran.'

'McMahon's handy for the Lasswade Broadway shop,' Fulton said. 'It's in his area.'

'I agree,' Knox said. 'And Wallace's near to the one at Colinton. If he's really gone AWOL, Macintosh might have Moran take his place.'

'Right,' Fulton said. 'How'd you want to play it?'

'Just stake out the shops for now, Bill. Low-key. You at Lasswade Road, Mark at Colinton. Use your iPhones – video anything interesting.'

'Righto, boss.'

* * *

Kaimes Green Court was a three-storey block near a play area, part of an open stretch of parkland on the edge of the estate. Knox reversed his car into a nearby bay, and he and McCann entered number 25, climbed stairs to the first floor, and located Flat 8. Seeing no buzzer, Knox rapped on the door, which was answered a moment later by a woman with her hair in curlers.

'Yes?' she said.

'DI Knox and DS McCann,' Knox said, showing her his warrant card. 'We'd like to speak to Tommy Kennedy.'

The woman gave a little sigh, ushered them in, and gestured to a flight of stairs leading off the hallway. 'Up there, the room facing you.'

'You're Mrs Kennedy?' Knox asked.

'No,' the woman replied. 'Mary Halliday, Jenny's sister. She's at the doctor's, picking up a prescription for depression.' She raised her eyes towards the upper floor. 'Heaven knows, with a laddie like that, she needs them.'

McCann indicated the stairs. 'The door facing, you said?'

The woman nodded. 'Aye,' she said. 'Give it a good hard knock. More than likely the bugger'll have his headphones on.'

The detectives ascended the stairs and McCann knocked on the door. Receiving no answer, she rapped again, harder. A moment later they heard the pad of footsteps. The door opened, and a youth in his late teens stared at them in surprise. 'Who are you?' he said.

'Tommy Kennedy?' Knox asked.

'Aye,' he said, then looked beyond them to the hallway below, where his aunt stood with her arms folded. 'They're polis, Tommy,' she called out. 'Getting to be a habit, isn't it?'

Kennedy scowled at her. 'Piss off,' he said.

His aunt threw up her arms in a gesture of resignation and addressed the detectives: 'See what I mean? Any wonder my sister takes pills?'

As she walked off in disgust, Knox motioned to the bedroom. 'We'd like a word, Tommy,' he said. 'We can talk in there or wait till we get to the station. Your choice.'

The youth gave him a sour look and stood aside. 'I spoke to your mate on Friday,' he said. 'He promised there'd be no charges as long as I cooperated. I told him everything he wanted to know.'

'You spoke to a police officer?' Knox asked.

'Aye, I told you. On Friday.'

'Where?'

'Here. Well, downstairs. In the living room.'

'What was the officer's name?'

'He didn't give his name. Flashed a card at my ma when she answered the door.'

'What did he look like?'

Kennedy studied Knox for a long moment. 'You've picked up the car, haven't you? He texted this morning, told me to do it tonight. He was lying, wasn't he?'

Knox and McCann exchanged confused glances, then Knox said, 'This officer, Tommy, I want you to describe him.'

Kennedy thought for a moment. 'I dunno, heavyish; going bald.'

'How old?'

'Fifties, I think.'

'He was here on Friday – what time?'

'Early afternoon.'

'Between one and two?'

'About then.'

'Where did you talk? Downstairs, or here in your room?'

'Downstairs, in the living room. He told my ma to leave, said he wanted to speak to me on my own.'

'Right, Tommy,' Knox said. 'Now, this is important. I want you to tell me exactly what he said.'

Kennedy sat on the edge of his bed and said nothing. Knox was about to ask him again, when he said, 'Your mate told me he'd checked CCTV at the chemist's. Saw me walking out of the crescent seconds after Smeaton was shot. Knew I'd phoned to let Shug know he was in his garden. It was easy to double-check my mobile signal, he said, and could verify it. I'd be done for aiding and abetting, get locked up for years. If I confirmed Shug killed Smeaton, though, he'd keep quiet about my involvement. It was Wallace he was after. He'd make sure I was kept out of it.'

'Paterson told you that – the detective?'

'Aye,' Kennedy said. 'Wanted to know exactly how I knew Shug, and how the hit was organised.'

'What did you tell him?'

'That I met him through my big brother, Rab, who owned a lockup in Gracemount. He was moving to Penicuik, put an ad on Gumtree. I was with Rab when Shug agreed to buy the lockup. We got pally, and I mentioned I'd done time in a youth offenders' for nicking cars. Told me last week he'd something coming up and needed a reliable motor. Offered five hundred if I'd get it for him.'

'The BMW?'

'Aye. Found it at Sainsbury's in Cameron Toll on Tuesday afternoon. Didn't have to do the locks, hot-wire the car or anything. The woman driver left it with the keys in the ignition. Couldn't believe my luck.'

'You garaged it at the lockup?'

'Aye. Phoned Shug who came here and picked up the keys, gave me an envelope with £500.'

'When was this?'

'Wednesday. Shug phoned me later that night, told me to be at Kaimes Green Crescent at 3pm on Thursday. He said Smeaton was known to do his garden then and I'd to confirm he was there. Told me after the hit he'd leave the Beamer in Kaimes Green Grove – the same cul-de-sac where he'd left it overnight. Said he'd switch to his own car and leave the area. The bottom end of the Grove's quiet – only a few pensioner houses in the street. I was to pick it up that night and take it back to the lockup.'

'And did you?'

'Aye. Shug said he'd wait a couple of days and phone, get me to take it to a bit of waste ground at Burdiehouse and set it alight. Told me he'd drop off an envelope with another five hundred once the job was done.'

'You told all this to Paterson?'

'Aye.'

'What did he say?'

'Not to do anything. Wait till he got in touch. He'd send me a text message to torch it later.' Kennedy nodded to his iPhone, which was on the bedside table. 'The message I got this morning.'

Knox reached into his pocket and took out an evidence bag. 'I'll need to take your phone, Tommy,' he said. 'And I'm sorry, but Paterson lied about keeping you out of it. What I can promise, though, is that if you repeat what you've just said at the station, I'll recommend bail and inform the court about your cooperation.'

Kennedy gave Knox a disconsolate look. 'But you're still charging me?'

'We can't avoid charges for theft of the car, Tommy,' Knox said. 'But I'll do everything in my power to make sure aiding and abetting is reduced to a lesser charge. I'll tell the court you were coerced by Wallace and that you cooperated willingly. Likely it'll mean you'll serve only months, not years – okay?'

Kennedy appeared slightly more mollified. 'Okay,' he said.

Chapter Twenty-two

'We were lucky,' Fulton was saying. 'I caught sight of McMahon within the first half-hour of getting here. Mark did better, spotted Moran minutes after he parked.'

Officers from nearby Howdenhall Police Station had just taken Kennedy into custody, and Knox and McCann had arrived back at the car when Fulton rang.

'The Lasswade Drive shop has a rear entrance,' he continued, 'so McMahon drove round the back. He must have forgotten something, though, because he stopped for a minute when he drove out again. Went back inside, came out with a package, and opened the boot. I'd a clear view from where I was parked. Watched him place it beside a dozen others.'

'And Mark?' Knox asked.

'Phoned a short while ago. Told me the Megane came to a stop in front of *Rosalind's* Colinton branch, where Moran entered and retrieved a black bin bag. He tossed it on the back seat and drove off. Mark says he was in and out in less than a minute.'

'You managed video clips?'

'Aye, boss. Everything's on tape.'

'Good work,' Knox said. 'One thing we know; whatever they picked up, it wasn't flowers.'

'Will Steele mount a raid now?' Fulton asked.

'Not right away,' Knox said. 'Likely he'll hang fire until Northumbria Police have apprehended Levy.'

'Aye, of course,' Fulton said. 'What I can't understand is how his undercover guys didn't pick up on the shops when they were surveilling McMahon and Wallace. I thought they were tailing them?'

'Only since Levy arrived and Wallace went missing. Prior to that they were setting up the sting. Never actually followed anyone until Hammond tailed Levy along the bypass, and Skinner witnessed him catch up with McMahon at Morrisons.'

'Right,' Fulton said. 'You want us to head back to Gayfield Square?'

'Aye, Bill. There's been a development at this end I'll tell you about later. I'm going to phone Steele at St Leonards and set up a meet. You and Mark head back to the office meantime, upload the flower shop videos to the computer. We'll see you later this afternoon.'

'Boss.'

Knox keyed Steele's number and the DCS answered moments later. 'Knox,' he said. 'How did it go with Kennedy?'

'He confirmed that Wallace shot Smeaton, sir. And confessed to stealing the car Wallace used.'

'You've ordered him into custody?'

'Yes, sir. He's on his way to Gayfield Square now.' A pause. 'But there's a bit more to it than that. Something I'd like to explain in person.'

'Of course,' Steele said. 'I'm still at St Leonards. DS Skinner and DS Hammond are with me.'

'And DI Paterson?'

'He's just stepped out of the office for a minute,' Steele said. 'But he'll be here when you get back.'

'Fine, sir. DS McCann and I will be with you in fifteen minutes.'

* * *

When Knox and McCann arrived at St Leonards, Steele greeted them with the news that Wallace's body had been found. 'DCI Stan Osmond from Leith Police Station just briefed me,' he told them. 'Wallace's girlfriend let herself into his flat in Manderston Street and discovered him in the living room. From what Osmond has been able to piece together, Wallace had made an attempt to retrieve a gun from the drawer of a drinks cabinet before he met his end.

'He'd a Glock pistol in his right hand – tried to use it, by the look of things. Same weapon used in Smeaton's murder, incidentally. Pathologists at Gartcosh have removed the two bullets that killed him – one in the upper abdomen, the other in the heart – which ballistics say came from a Beretta automatic.'

'You know where Levy is?' Knox asked.

Hammond and Skinner were hunched over their computers and Paterson was looking on. Steele nodded in their direction and replied, 'We're checking local council and Traffic Scotland's CCTVs. Picked up Levy's vehicles at Joppa, heading in the direction of the A1.' He gestured towards Hammond and added, 'Steve?'

'They're on the A1 now, sir,' Hammond said. 'Last sighting three minutes ago near Haddington.'

Steele nodded. 'Naturally, we'll monitor progress but won't act, except to make sure Northumbria Police is informed. DCS Hyde contacted me earlier to say they've been keeping an eye on Levy's farm at Cleadon – and discovered something interesting. Last night an articulated lorry lettered with the name of a Dutch flower exporter arrived. The driver took the vehicle into Levy's yard, unhitched the trailer, hooked up an empty one parked a short distance away, and drove out again. Undercover officers followed it to North Shields terminal, where it boarded a ferry for Amsterdam. They've staked out his place and are waiting for his return.'

'That's their cover,' Knox said. 'Flowers.' He told Steele about Fulton and Hathaway's surveillance of Macintosh's shops, and added, 'We're ninety-nine per cent sure McMahon and Moran were picking up drugs.'

'It's coming together,' Steele said. 'Finally. Levy's importing from the Netherlands, using the flower business as a screen.'

'You'll wait on the outcome of DCS Hyde's raid before you move on Macintosh?' Knox asked.

'Of course,' Steele agreed. He paused for a long moment, then added, 'You said on the phone you'd something to discuss?'

Knox looked at Paterson, who was sitting at his desk twirling a pencil in his fingers. 'DI Paterson might want to comment,' Knox said. 'Because what I am about to say concerns him.'

'Go on,' Steele said.

'As I told you, sir, Mr Purvis gave me the lead. Kennedy had been wearing a distinctive red baseball cap on the day Smeaton was murdered. Purvis recalled seeing him, and later discussed the shooting with a teenager who delivers his papers. The lad told him he knew where Kennedy lived.'

'Which is how you got on to him?'

'Yes, sir. And discovered he'd already been interviewed.' Knox paused. 'By DI Paterson.'

Steele turned to face Paterson. 'Is this true?'

Paterson put down the pencil and gave Knox a look of contempt. 'I spoke to some boys in the area, sir,' he said. 'Who told me they'd seen Kennedy wave to the BMW driver as the car drove past. When I followed up, I found it to be tittle-tattle. Kennedy was nowhere near when it happened.'

'Really?' Knox said. 'You didn't check CCTV at a local chemist?'

'I looked at their recordings,' Paterson said smugly. 'Kennedy isn't on them, nor is the BMW.'

Knox gave a nod of comprehension. 'So it was subterfuge, a ploy used to get him to admit involvement?'

'I don't know what you're talking about.'

'You *did* talk to some local kids,' Knox said, 'who, when you mentioned a red baseball cap, pointed you in Kennedy's direction.'

'Rubbish.'

'Is it? What about the BMW; the lockup? Tommy made a full confession and you swept it under the carpet. Why?'

'Wait a minute, Knox,' Steele said. 'You'd better repeat what Kennedy said to you.'

Knox motioned towards Paterson. 'Exactly what he'd told DI Paterson, sir. Wallace befriended Kennedy when he bought a lockup in Gracemount from his brother. Discovered he'd previous for car theft and persuaded him to steal the car he used on the day Smeaton was shot. Got him to hide it out of sight in the lockup afterwards. He was to wait a couple of days, then set it alight on a stretch of waste ground. Kennedy told all this to Paterson, who warned him to keep quiet. Said no charges would be brought against him if he did.'

'Kennedy's trying it on, man,' Paterson said. 'That's a complete pack of lies.'

'Is it?' Knox said. 'When you spoke to him you didn't emphasise that your only interest was Wallace? Insist he do nothing about the car meantime? That you'd contact him when it was safe to get rid of it?'

'Of course not,' Paterson said. 'What would I gain by doing that?'

'Money,' Knox said. 'If you were blackmailing Wallace.'

'That's a serious charge, Knox,' Steele said.

'I know it is, sir,' Knox said. 'But how else do you account for Wallace's disappearance? Because not only did

Paterson let him know we were we onto him, he also told him Levy was on his way here.'

'You've taken leave of your senses,' Paterson said.

'Have I?' Knox replied, and turned to Steele. 'DI Paterson made a deal with Wallace, sir, I'd bet my life on it. If you check his bank account I'm sure you'll find evidence.'

Paterson raised his hands in supplication. 'Really, sir,' he said to Steele. 'This is an outrage. Knox has gone mad. There's nothing whatsoever to support such allegations.'

Steele gave Knox a grave look. 'You're skating on thin ice, Knox. You'd better have something to back this up.'

Knox dipped his head in acknowledgement. 'I have, sir.' Then to Paterson he said, 'You're claiming everything Kennedy told me is lies?'

Paterson glared at him. 'I am,' he said. 'Kennedy's havering. And so are you.'

'You didn't send him a text this morning, telling him to get rid of the BMW?'

'No,' Paterson said. 'The very suggestion is preposterous.'

Knox took a pair of nitrile gloves from his pocket, put them on, then nodded to McCann, who took an evidence pouch from her handbag and handed it to him. Knox extracted a mobile phone, navigated to the text folder, and addressed Steele.

'This iPhone belongs to Kennedy, sir,' Knox said. 'We took it from him earlier.' He pointed to the message. 'And this is the last text he received.' Knox highlighted the text, and continued, 'It says: "Torch the car tonight. Wait till late. Make sure nobody sees you."'

Knox clicked on the text, brought up the sender's number and pressed *call*. A moment or two passed, then Paterson's mobile began to ring.

Knox pointed towards Paterson, who automatically reached for the phone in his pocket.

'And as we can hear,' Knox continued, 'DI Paterson owns the phone that sent it.'

He ended the call, and Paterson's mobile immediately ceased ringing. Paterson's face crumpled, and both Hammond and Skinner turned, staring daggers at their colleague.

'DI Paterson,' Steele said with a look of contempt, 'you are under arrest on charges of wilfully undermining a police operation for financial advantage. You will be remanded in custody until our Complaints and Conduct Division can investigate. DS Hammond, DS Skinner – take Paterson to the desk sergeant, please. Remand him in custody and register a formal charge.'

Steele's undercover officers sprang to their feet and took Paterson by the arms. As he was led from the room, Steele turned to Knox. 'As I mentioned earlier, I've had misgivings about Paterson for some time. However, sometimes it takes an outsider to smell something rotten under your nose. I'm in your debt, Knox.'

'Sir,' Knox said.

Steele indicated the screen of the computer on Hammond's desk, which showed a view from a CCTV camera near Alnwick, and had just pinged as the PNC system recognised the registration number of Levy's Land Rover. 'Now, to business,' he said. 'Time to nail these drug runners and put this operation to bed.'

Chapter Twenty-three

It was almost dusk when the Land Rover and Mitsubishi passed through the village of Cleadon and covered the last few miles to Levy's farm. The vehicles came to a T-junction, indicated left and drove for another five minutes, then turned right into a gravel-tracked road and carried on for another two hundred yards.

They slowed as the track opened onto a wide rectangular courtyard with a number of buildings at either side, with a large field situated at the end. A row of cottages on the right had been renovated and upgraded into one dwelling. Beyond this lay a former stable block, converted into garages. Immediately opposite were two large storage sheds, alongside the first of which a trailer was parked. It bore the name: *Steffen Meijer, Flower Exporter, Amsterdam.*

The Land Rover and Mitsubishi stopped and Levy, Musgrave and Nevins exited. Levy pointed to the container and turned to the others. 'Good,' he said. 'Jacob's been.' He nodded to the garages and added, 'Right, lads. Let's get the flowers and gear unloaded and stowed in the cool sheds. Then we can get our feet up. Baz, Andy; fetch the forklifts, I'll unlock the container.'

'Boss,' Musgrave and Nevins chorused, and crossed the yard to the garages.

Levy, meanwhile, took a bunch of keys from his pocket, selected one and unlocked a padlock, and pulled open the container doors.

The interior was packed with wooden pallets, on which pairs of identical flat cardboard boxes were stacked eight high and secured with plastic ties. On the floor of the container, the load was arranged four pallets across and eighteen deep.

As the forklifts rumbled into position, Levy pointed to the rear. 'Usual procedure,' he said. 'Nearest two rows first, then the rows on either side front to back. Once we get a bit more room, you can use a forklift to lift the pallet jack onto the container floor and I'll draw out the ones that need hooks for the deck spaces.'

* * *

Two hundred yards distance from the farm, in a copse in the middle of the field, DCS Alan Hyde and DCI Gary Winters of Northumbria Police Narcotics Division surveyed the scene through powerful night-vision binoculars. They saw Musgrave and Nevins remove the nearest stack from the container, then raise a pallet jack with a forklift, which Levy used to move the boxes within.

'They'll take care of the sides and back first,' Hyde said. 'The pallets with the drugs will have been placed in the middle.'

'How many do you reckon, sir?' Winters asked.

'Around a dozen, I think. We'll see them get special attention as they're taken out.'

Winters nodded towards the farm. 'The teams are in place?'

'Aye,' Hyde said. 'One out of sight at the end of the field. The other parked in a lane fifty yards away. All armed response – just waiting for the signal.' Hyde thumbed the focus wheel of his binoculars. 'There,' he said, 'the pair with Levy have taken poles from the shed.'

Winters refocused his own glasses and watched Musgrave and Nevins carry two long poles with hooks to the trailer, which they inserted into the forklift arm spaces of the nearest pallets. He saw them extract flat objects similar to deep baking trays, and stack them beside the container.

'The drugs,' Hyde explained. 'Hidden in the pallet decks, where the forklift arms go. The spaces are sleeved with copper, and the drugs packed in plastic trays near the rear. A snug fit, but it works; enables forklifts and pallet jacks to insert far enough to lift the load. When flowers are placed on the trailer, they use the jacks to position the pallets with drugs in the centre. This, together with the copper sleeves, makes it near impossible for port authority X-ray machines to detect them.'

'Look, sir,' Winters said. 'They're moving the last of the consignment now.'

Hyde trained his glasses on the trailer and saw Levy use the pallet jack to bring the final two stacks of flowers to the rear. Musgrave and Nevins then repeated the process with the pole hooks – removing and stacking the plastic inserts, then laying the poles aside and using forklifts to take down the pallets.

'You're right, Gary,' Hyde said. 'They're about done.' He reached for his radio and pressed the *transmit* button. 'Hyde to all units,' he said. 'Go, go, go. I say again: go, go, go.'

As Levy jumped from the container, he and his cohorts were blinded by lights coming from the direction of the field. At almost the same time two Range Rovers roared into the yard, their wheels spraying gravel as they ground to a halt with their headlights on full beam. The trio stood immobilised as a loudspeaker sounded: 'Armed Police. Stay where you are and do not move. These premises are surrounded. I repeat: armed police. Stay where you are!'

The three watched as officers exited the vehicles and trained the muzzles of Heckler and Koch MP5 machine pistols in their direction. Levy glanced towards the field and saw a further two Range Rovers. A dozen more officers faced them, weapons aimed.

Levy glanced at his companions. 'Outnumbered and outflanked, guys,' he said. 'Time to give it up.' Then, to the group of officers in the yard, 'Okay, bonny lads, we know when we're beat.' He gave a thin smile and nodded to the cottages. 'We've been on the road all day, though. Don't suppose there's time for a cuppa?'

The lead officer in the yard, a sergeant, dipped the barrel of his gun and said, 'I want the three of you on the ground. Now! Face down. No sudden movements.'

As he and his mates complied, Levy shrugged and said, 'I take it that's a no, then?'

The sergeant nodded to several of his colleagues who went to the men, who now lay prostrate. The officers drew their arms behind their backs and cuffed their wrists.

After they were secured and pulled to their feet, a dark blue Vauxhall Insignia saloon drove into the yard and DCI Winters and DCS Hyde exited. 'Everything okay, Sergeant?' Hyde said.

The officer pointed to a pallet alongside the container. 'My lads checked over there, sir. Fourteen trays, each packed with two bags of drugs. We had a quick peek, looks to be heroin and cocaine, an almost fifty-fifty mix.'

'Quite a haul,' Hyde said.

Levy, standing between two officers a short distance away, glanced at Hyde. 'Didn't want to run out,' he said with a snort. 'Coming up to our busy season.'

'You'll be Mr Levy?' Hyde said.

'Guilty,' Levy said.

Hyde gave a little smile. 'A word you'll be hearing from a judge in the not too distant future, Mr Levy,' he said. Then to the sergeant, 'He was carrying?'

The officer nodded. 'A Beretta M9, tucked into his belt.'

'Get it off to Gartcosh, will you, Sergeant? Our friends up there are seeking a match for a recent homicide in Edinburgh.'

Levy glanced at Musgrave and Nevins, standing nearby with their escorts, and addressed Hyde, 'Who grassed?'

'Pardon?' Hyde said.

'Who put you on to us?'

'Why, you did, Mr Levy,' Hyde replied, then motioned towards Musgrave and Nevins. 'Or maybe one of your friends did.'

Levy gave him a look of disbelief and shook his head. 'No chance.'

Hyde pointed to several empty pallets stacked nearby. 'I believe you have a timber merchant near Cleadon who disposes of your damaged pallets?'

'So?' Levy said.

'Apparently you were a bit negligent the last time he was here.' Hyde pointed to the last pallets unloaded, the ones he and Winters had seen forklifted from the trailer. 'The pallets with the drugs, have them specially made, do you? The ones with the lead lining?'

Levy shrugged but said nothing.

'Well, it seems either you or one of your colleagues included a damaged pallet with the lining intact. Unusual to find a lump of lead in the deck of one of those things, don't you agree?'

Levy made a face, but remained silent.

'Well, unfortunately for you, the timber merchant had a visit from an off-duty police officer last week,' Hyde continued. 'He was in the process of making a hut for his garden and on the lookout for materials. Spotted the sleeve, put two and two together, and brought it to our attention.' A pause. 'The little things, Mr Levy. It's the little things that catch us out.'

At that moment a police van pulled into the yard and
Hyde gestured towards it and addressed the sergeant. 'The
paddy wagon,' he said. 'Help Mr Levy and his friends
aboard and escort them to the station. We'll carry out a
more detailed inventory here and prefer charges later.'

Chapter Twenty-four

Knox and his team were finishing for the day when DCS Steele arrived in the office. 'Glad I caught you,' he said. 'Thought you'd like to be brought up to date.'

'Levy was caught?' Knox asked.

'Pretty much red-handed,' Steele replied. 'I told you Northumbria Police were staking out his farm?'

'Yes, sir. You said a lorry had called at his place, left a container, and picked up an empty one.'

'Well, DCS Hyde and his officers waited until Levy and his pals returned and witnessed them empty it. Twelve kilos of heroin and sixteen kilos of uncut cocaine – hidden in the decks of the pallets.'

'Wow,' Fulton said. 'That's a fair amount of marching powder.'

'Quite,' Steele said.

'Levy,' Knox said, 'did he give DCS Hyde and his men any trouble?'

'Apparently not,' Steele replied. 'I think he was taken by surprise.'

'The weapon used to murder Wallace,' Knox asked, 'they were able to recover it?'

Steele nodded. 'A Beretta M9. On its way to our ballistics people at Gartcosh.'

'And Macintosh?'

'I was about to say. Hammond and Skinner led two teams, raided his shops a little over an hour ago.' Steele motioned to Fulton and Hathaway. 'Your lads were right. A considerable quantity of drugs was found at both premises. We're not sure if the staff were aware that Macintosh and his cohorts were storing them. We've closed the shops anyway, taken them in for questioning.'

Steele paused then added, 'We found the man himself at St John's Road. He was taken to West End Police Station, charged there. The others were rounded up and taken into custody, too. Moran was at Macintosh's house in Colinton, McMahon at his place in Captain's Road. The pair who were seen by my men – Reid and Allison – were brought in for questioning. Doubtful if they'll be charged with anything, but we'll hold them a while, see what they can tell us.'

'You told us Levy was being supplied from the Netherlands,' Knox said. 'Any likelihood of running down his source at that end?'

'Good question, Knox. Yes, DCS Hyde tells me they've been in touch with the Dutch police through Interpol. They've checked CCTV records of the vehicle his men followed to North Shields terminal. Hyde thinks there's a fair chance of catching the ringleaders.'

Steele paused and indicated DCI Warburton's office in the corner of the room. 'I'm just about to pop in and see your boss, thank him for his cooperation.' He nodded to Knox and the others. 'Meantime I'd also like to thank you all for a job well done.'

After Steele departed for Warburton's office, Knox checked his watch. 'Well, I think we can call it a day,' he said. 'Bill, Mark, you managed to finish the paperwork on Clare Tomkins?'

'Yes, boss,' Fulton said. 'We received a formal report from Professor Dott at the Royal Edinburgh. I've sent it together with our own to the procurator fiscal and a copy to head office.'

'Good,' Knox said, then nodded to McCann. 'Arlene and I will complete our report on the Macintosh case in the morning. We all can get off home.'

As Fulton and Hathaway said goodnight and left the office, McCann shrugged on her coat and took her handbag from the back of her chair. 'You went out on a limb at St Leonards, boss, if you don't mind me saying,' she said. 'What convinced you that Paterson was blackmailing Wallace?'

'A strong hunch,' Knox replied, grinning. 'That and the fact that fire tenders were nowhere near St John's Road yesterday afternoon.'

McCann broke into a smile. 'You checked?'

Knox nodded. 'Uh-huh,' he said. 'Which meant there was only one reason Paterson hadn't followed Wallace. He'd already seen him.'

'To arrange a little extortion,' McCann said. 'The devious bugger.' She slung her handbag over her shoulder and headed for the door. 'Okay, boss, see you in the morning. Night.'

'Goodnight, Arlene.'

* * *

Knox let himself into his flat, went into the living room, and crossed to the drinks cabinet and poured himself a large measure of Glenmorangie. He placed the glass on a nearby table, took a remote and turned on the sound system, then he sat in an armchair and let the music waft over him.

Debussy's *Clair de Lune* – it had been one of Yvonne's favourites. He'd been playing it a lot lately.

It had been less than two months, but he was still finding it hard to come to terms with her loss.

He swallowed a third of the glass's contents, placed the tumbler on the table, and settled back. Soon the warming liquor took effect.

His eyelids became heavier and heavier…

Yvonne was wearing a bright floral dress. She leaned over and kissed him. He could smell the perfume on her neck. He opened his eyes and saw her – she smiled and caressed his cheek.

'It's strange you should be wearing a floral dress,' he said. 'I've been thinking a lot about flowers lately.'

'I know, darling, I know. That's why I wore it.'

He gazed at her again. She looked just as she had the last time he'd kissed her. The night she returned to her flat. The night she…

He felt tears prick his eyes. 'I miss you, Yvonne,' he said. 'I miss you very much.'

She caressed his cheek again and said, 'I know, you do, Jack, darling, I know you do. But I don't want you to worry. I'm fine, Jack, really I am.'

She began to echo and repeat – 'Really I am, really I am…'

Her voice was replaced by a strident ringing.

He sat bolt upright in the armchair and was awake again, a sheen of sweat on his forehead. The ringing persisted. He glanced at the table and saw his iPhone vibrating and the screen flashing.

He muted the sound system and picked up the mobile. 'Hello?'

'Mr Knox?'

'Yeah. Who's that?'

'Bernard Macintosh. I'm calling from West End Police Station. They allowed me two calls. The first was to my solicitor.'

'How did you get my number?'

'You left your card. At Gillespie Road, first time you spoke to me.'

'Why are you calling?'

'I read a report in the *Daily Record*. Concerns Derek Tate, Mr Knox. He committed suicide, but you probably know that. I got to thinking about what I said to you – how other convicts feel about men who kill women?'

'I remember,' Knox said.

'I just wanted you to know I had nothing to do with it – Tate killing himself, I mean. Just in case you think I did. Tell you the truth, Mr Knox, I considered it. Even asked Roddy to get me the number of one of the inmates at Saughton, Pete Gifford.

'I took no action, though. Roddy asked me later if I called him, but I told him I hadn't. I didn't tell him why I wanted Gifford's number, by the way.

'He told me afterwards he'd called Pete himself – I think they'd a blether about old times, when Gifford was getting out, that sort of thing. Anyway, after I saw the *Record* piece I got to thinking about what I'd said to you, wondered if you'd think I had any connection with Tate's death. Why I phoned, Mr Knox. To assure you I hadn't.'

'The thought *had* crossed my mind, to be honest,' Knox said.

'I thought it might,' Macintosh said. 'I can only repeat, though, I had nothing to do with it. I hope you believe me.'

'I've no reason to disbelieve you,' Knox said.

'Just wanted to set the record straight, that's all.'

'Okay,' Knox said. 'I appreciate it.'

'I didn't say when I spoke to you, Mr Knox, because one normally doesn't in such circumstances. But I sent a bouquet of flowers to DC Mason's funeral.'

Knox was taken aback. 'Well, Mr Macintosh, you've my belated thanks.'

'Thank you for listening, Mr Knox. And goodbye.'

'Goodbye.'

Knox put down the phone and his thoughts went again to the dream of Yvonne and the floral dress she'd been wearing. And the coincidence it had been Macintosh ringing about Tate that had awoken him.

And the dream: it had been all too real – almost as if she'd been in the room with him. When he'd told her he missed her, she'd replied, '*I know you do. But I don't want you to worry. I'm fine, Jack, really I am.*'

He could still hear her voice as he settled back the armchair: '*I'm fine, Jack, really I am.*' He took a long sip of whisky, restarted the music, and felt better than he had in many weeks.

The End

List of Characters

Officers based in Edinburgh:

Detective Inspector Jack Knox – head of the Major Incident Inquiry team based at Gayfield Square Police Station, Edinburgh

Detective Sergeant Bill Fulton – Knox's partner, second member of the Major Inquiry Team

Detective Sergeant Arlene McCann – third member of the Major Inquiry Team

Detective Constable Mark Hathaway – fourth member of the Major Inquiry Team

Detective Chief Inspector Ronald Warburton – senior detective at Gayfield Square Police Station

Detective Inspector Edward (Ed) Murray – forensics officer based in Edinburgh

Detective Sergeant Elizabeth (Liz) Beattie – forensics officer and Murray's assistant

Detective Inspector John Madden – officer based at Torphichen Place (West End) Police Station

Detective Sergeant Kirsty Gray – officer based at Torphichen Place (West End) Police Station

Gartcosh Narcotics Division officers:

Detective Chief Superintendent Andrew Steele – officer in charge, Narcotics Division
Detective Sergeant Keith Skinner – undercover narcotics officer
Detective Sergeant Steve Hammond – undercover narcotics officer
Detective Inspector Niall Paterson – case officer, Narcotics Division

Northumbria Police officers:

Detective Chief Superintendent Alan Hyde – officer in charge, Northumbria Police Narcotics Division
Detective Chief Inspector Gary Winters – DCS Hyde's assistant

Others:

Alexander Turley – pathologist
Clare Tomkins – murder victim
Giles Abercrombie – solicitor
Mr David Graham – rambler who discovered the murder victim
Mrs Ellie Graham – David Graham's wife
Fiona Baird – Clare Tomkins' room-mate and friend
Sofia Adler – Clare Tomkins' room-mate and friend
Sandrine Cudlipp – friend of Clare Tomkins' in adjoining dorm
Rebecca Ryan – friend of Clare Tomkins' in adjoining dorm
Louise Jardine – Rebecca Ryan's friend
Fraser McCauley – Clare Tomkins' first boyfriend
David Martin – Clare Tomkins' second boyfriend

Clive Parker – David Martin's room-mate

Ms Rhona Adams – Glassel House block supervisor

Bernard Macintosh – regional drugs distributor

Norman Smeaton – murdered in drug dealer's internecine dispute

Lisa Smeaton – Norman Smeaton's wife

Sandy Purvis – Norman Smeaton's neighbour

Tommy McKenzie – Hugh Wallace's lookout

Hugh (Shug) Wallace – drug dealer

Angus (Gus) McMahon – drug dealer

Roddy Moran – Bernard Macintosh's chauffeur/bodyguard

Sammy Reid – Moran's ex-cellmate

Albert (Bert) Allison – Sammy Reid's mate

Paddy Malachy – Saughton Prison inmate

Lionel Levy – Newcastle drug dealer

Basil (Baz) Musgrave – Lionel Levy's enforcer

Andrew (Andy) Nevins – Lionel Levy's enforcer

Mrs Grace Lowrie – Rebecca Ryan's foster parent

Dr Gavin Ross – Royal Edinburgh Hospital psychiatrist

Professor Alistair Dott – consultant psychiatrist, Royal Edinburgh Hospital

If you enjoyed this book, please let others know by leaving a quick review on Amazon. Also, if you spot anything untoward in the paperback, get in touch. We strive for the best quality and appreciate reader feedback.

editor@thebookfolks.com

www.thebookfolks.com

MORE FICTION BY ROBERT McNEILL

All the books in this series of DI Jack Knox detective novels are free on Kindle Unlimited and available in paperback!

The Innocent and the Dead (Book 1)

One girl is found dead – strangled in the woods. Another, the daughter of a rich, well-connected businessman, is kidnapped. Unassuming detective Jack Knox must solve these two cases. But the Edinburgh crime-solver will have a hard time getting his superiors to accept his unconventional methods. Will he gamble too much?

Murder at Flood Tide (Book 2)

When a young woman's body is found, the nature of her killing leads detectives to believe the murderer may strike again soon. The race is on to find him, but he has covered his tracks well. DI Jack Knox's investigation is impeded by a disgruntled officer from another force. Can he solve the case and collar the culprit?

Dead of Night (Book 3)

When a philandering French college lecturer is killed and unceremoniously dumped in a canal, DI Jack Knox soon discovers there is no shortage of spurned lovers and jealous husbands who might have done it. He sets about collaring the culprit, but will his efforts be thwarted by unfair complaints made about the investigation?

Noughts and Crosses (Book 4)

After defrauding wealthy investors of a serious amount of money, a financial advisor is found dead on a residential street in Edinburgh. DI Jack Knox must tread carefully to follow the trail that might lead to the killer. But will the events that ensue prove too much even for him?

Confession to Murder (Book 6)

After a man confesses in church that he has killed a girl, having wrangled with his conscience the priest tells the police. It would be easy for them to dismiss the confessor as a crank, but DI Knox has a hunch the victim could be a young Canadian tourist who has gone missing. Yet with few other leads, it will take brilliant detective work to catch the killer.

Don't Cry, Darling (Book 7)

The Edinburgh major crimes team is on high alert after a shooting at a card game leaves three people dead. But the officers must divide their focus when the daughter of a prominent figure goes missing. Can DI Knox catch her abductor before the unthinkable happens, and stop a dangerous killer in his tracks?

OTHER TITLES OF INTEREST

CATFISH by Sadie Norman

It is not without some malice that rookie detective Anna McArthur is called "crazy" by her colleagues. She certainly tends to act first and think later. But when Anna discovers the body of a murdered woman who has "catfish" carved into her chest, she feels a personal duty to do everything she can to up her game and find the killer.

CRIMES OF THE FALLEN by James Andrew

When DI John Belivat is called to the scene of a murdered woman, left naked on the seafront of a Scottish town, it brings back all his fears about the fate of his own missing daughter. He focuses on the victim, trying to establish her identity. But only after another body is found will the detective be able to piece together a motive and find a killer.

All FREE with Kindle Unlimited and available in paperback.

*Sign up to our mailing list to find out about new releases
and special offers!*

www.thebookfolks.com